LINDA COGGIN

HOT
KEY
BOOKS

First published in Great Britain in 2015 by
HOT KEY BOOKS
80–81 Wimpole St, London W1G 9RE
www.hotkeybooks.com

A CIP catalogue record for this book is
available from the British Library.

ISBN: 978–1–4714–0318–7
also available as an ebook

Typeset   on using Atomik ePublisher

Print   and bound by Clays Ltd, St Ives Plc

Hot Key Bo   Publishing Fiction,
                                          pany

                                                  s.co.uk

ALSO BY LINDA COGGIN

The Boy with the Tiger's Heart

For Chloë

Chapter 1

When my death came it was swift. Swift as a racing horse. It wasted no time. Like a conjuring trick. One moment I was in the car, the next on the road, and then I wasn't anywhere. When I awoke I was slouched in a chair in a room with yellow paint peeling off the walls and a table at the far end. Yes. My death was as fleet as the wind. Meteoric, you might say. Mercurial, like quick silver. No floating above the body looking down on the grieving relatives. It was snappy, prompt. It was *smart.*

It's funny, now I come to think of it. The man

who was driving the car always had a fear of horses. He was so afraid of them he would never get on one, nor pat one on the neck, nor let their lovely soft muzzles blow in his face. I know all this because the man driving the car was my dad, and my mum had told me how scared of horses he was.

'It's unreasonable, really,' she'd say. 'He's never had anything to do with them. It's not like he was kicked by one when he was small.'

And that is what's funny. Because the reason I ended up on the road was because a horse jumped over a hedge onto my dad's car as we were driving to the supermarket. So it had been a premonition. His fear of horses.

'You'd better hurry up, dear,' said someone at the table at the far end, 'or all the best jobs will be taken. We had a multiple coach crash just before you came in and most of the *qualified* jobs have gone.'

'Jobs?' I asked. 'Why do I need a job? I'm only twelve.'

'*Were* only twelve, dear,' the voice corrected.

'I've got you down as Daisy Fellows. Distinguishing features one blue eye and one green eye. Is that right?'

I nodded. I had always longed to have one of those old-fashioned passports that Mum had told me about. I'd never seen one, but Mum said they used to have a section for distinguishing marks. I thought whoever read it would have to look long into my eyes to make sure it was true and I would learn to perfect a blank stare so that they wouldn't be able to see into my soul. But they don't do that any more. The passport I got last year just had a little microchip in it that probably said everything there is to know about me, including my bad marks in the maths exam.

A woman was sorting out a pile of papers on the desk and she glanced at me every now and then.

'Really, my dear, you don't want to get *cold*. You must go while you can. A new baby is about to be born in Spitalfields. It's the only *qualified* job left. I think we've got about two minutes, so come and sign the form and then you must be off.'

'Off? I don't understand,' I said. 'I've only just arrived. And I don't even know where I am. Is this Heaven or something?'

'Heaven? Goodness, my dear. What an old-fashioned concept of death. You are in one of our Government-run Job Centres. You are a *soul*, are you not? Everyone who is born needs a soul. It's just a question of whose body you take up. Look upon it as rehousing.'

She was just about to hand me a form to sign when a telephone rang at her side. She picked it up.

'Oh dear. Really? What a shame. Thank you for letting me know.' The woman looked at me. 'The baby was stillborn. No need for you to go *there*.'

'Why is no one else here?' I asked. 'Six thousand three hundred and ninety people die per hour. I learnt that at school. Where are they all?'

'That's an old figure, my dear. Far more people die than that. But that's not the point. The point is we like to treat people as *individuals*. There are lots of rooms in the building, you know, and queues of people waiting to come in here.'

'What about my dad? He'll be here, won't he?'

'I don't know, dear – what's his name?'

'Dennis Fellows.'

The woman opened a drawer marked *F* and rifled through it. 'Fanshawe. Featherstone. Fielding. Can't see a *Dennis* Fellows; there's a Freddie Fellows – any relation?'

I shook my head.

'He can't be dead, then,' she said.

Good, I thought. Mum'll be pleased. Just me, then. No joint funeral. Thank goodness. I wouldn't want to be buried to something by the Beatles. I thought about it for a moment. It would've been fun to see who'd come to it – most of Year Eight, I guessed. I hoped Owen Taylor turned up and wept buckets for me. Of course, technically I wouldn't have had my funeral yet. I was probably still lying on the road, covered in a sheet. I expected there was a crowd of people. They always stop and stare at accidents. I wondered what had happened to the horse. Perhaps it was in the queue outside, waiting to come back as a hedgehog.

'So Mum was right about her theory of coming

back again as something else when you die?' I said. 'She was into Buddhism.'

'It's not about *religion*,' the woman said scornfully. 'It's about practicalities. Now you're getting cold, aren't you? I can see you shivering. We must hurry. Ah yes. You needn't sign any forms for this one – it's not a qualified job. Off you go, dear – through that door on the right.'

'But what's my – er . . . who, er – *what's my job? Who am I to become?*'

'There's a litter being born right now in a charming house. I'm sure you'll like it. They're nearly all out but I'll arrange for one to be stuck in the birth canal. That'll give you about three minutes to get there. Remember – *the door on the right!*'

I just had the handle in my hand when the door flew open. It definitely seemed like sky out there, and when I looked down, a jagged vent opened up and it felt as if something had grabbed hold of my legs. Too late, I realised – I had gone through the door on the left. Out of the corner of my eye I'd seen a notice – *Absolutely No Exit.*

I was meant to have gone through *the door on the right*. I found myself falling, falling. And it was as quick as the wind. It was snappy, prompt. It was *smart*.

As I fell I remember shouting out, 'What sort of litter? Am I going to be a pig? A cat? *A rat*?' But no one heard me and it wasn't until I could open my eyes twelve days later that I could see, perfectly well, that I had come back to Earth as a dog.

Chapter 2

'So which of these dear little puppies would you like, Cyril?' the woman in the alarmingly pink dress asks.

'Me! Me! Take me!' they all say, their little tails wagging.

Why? Who would want to go with a woman in a pink *acrylic dress*. I could just imagine her home. It would probably have pink furry seat covers on the loo.

I hide under the table.

Cyril picks up one of my brothers by the tail and he gives a loud yelp.

'Cyril! Don't do that. Now which one do you want?'

'Me! Me! Take me!' they all go again, jumping up and making themselves appear as adorable as possible.

'I want that one hiding under the table,' he says, getting down on his hands and knees and peering at me. I glare at him. He smells of sweets and socks.

'Urgh – look, Mum! It's got funny eyes. They're different colours. I don't want it after all.'

'I don't know, Cyril,' the woman says, looking under the table. 'It's rather sweet. Anyway, it's the only female. And I did say we'd get a girl. I don't want some boy dog running after everything that moves.'

Cyril lets out a wail. 'Don't want a girl. Want a boy to play football with.'

I growl at him.

'Cyril, it's just a *dog*. I'm sure you can throw a ball for it, but it won't be able to play football.'

'Actually, I *can* play football,' I tell them. 'I got into the all-girls' football team at my school.

I've scored literally *hundreds* of goals.' But they don't understand me.

'Oh look, the poor thing is *whimpering*. My mind is made up, Cyril. It's adorable.'

I never do get to see if they have pink furry covers on the loo because when they get me back they proudly show me my new home. A dog kennel – outside!

'I'm not sleeping in *that*,' I say. 'I want a basket, at least. And perhaps one of those nice tartan rugs or, even better, a *bean bag*. Now that *would* be comfy. I imagine I'll be doing a lot of lying around. I'm sure I wouldn't have been allowed to go with you if they'd known I was going to have to sleep *outside*!'

'I think she likes it,' the woman in the pink dress says. 'Come on, Cyril, we must leave her to rest. We'll come back and see her later.'

'Rest?' I say. 'I'm not an invalid!'

'I want to play football,' Cyril whines.

'So do I!'

'All in due course, Cyril. Lunchtime first. Spaghetti bolognaise.'

'I love spaghetti bolognaise,' I say, and jump up and down to get some attention. 'It's practically my favourite food – after Thai green curry.'

'I think she's telling us she needs to do pee-pee,' Cyril's mother answers. 'Go on, Cyril, go and put her on the newspaper in the yard and then we must go in and have our luncheon.'

Cyril grabs me by the neck and drags me, protesting, to the yard. Cyril's house looks much like everyone else's in the road. It has a neat square of grass, a garage with double doors and a little concrete area on which his mother has placed some pages from a newspaper. Dragging my heels, I reluctantly follow him. My mum had always advised me to take any opportunity I could to use a loo. 'Because you just don't know when or where you'll find another chance.'

As I stand over the paper my eye catches sight of the headline.

GIRL AND HORSE KILLED IN FATAL ROAD ACCIDENT. MAN LEFT PARALYSED. And there, smiling back at me, is my picture.

What on earth possessed them to use that

picture? My school photo! I look demented and about six years old. Why couldn't they have used that one taken on the beach in Turkey? The one with my hair looking particularly good – kind of windswept and interesting.

There is another picture of a mass of flowers and teddy bears that '*friends of Daisy have left at the spot where she was killed*'. I look at the date on the paper and see that it is about three months old. I've already been a dog for a quarter of a year.

After I recover from the thought of my school photo being seen by thousands of readers, I think of my poor dad being paralysed. I wonder how he and Mum are coping. I look back at the paper again. How could I possibly pee on *that*?

I am lying here. Waiting. Waiting to hear someone call my name. *Misty!* What sort of silly, airy-fairy name is *that*? It's not like I'm fluffy. I don't look like a Misty. I caught a glimpse of myself in the reflection of a puddle the other day. I've got quite sharp features. A long pointy nose and funny little ears that flop over at the top. But I can make them stand up when I feel like it, which is really cool.

So here I am, *waiting*. Waiting for someone to take me for a walk. I could take myself for a walk but I'm attached to this kennel. Not in a fond way but by a length of cord. And Cyril cannot be relied upon to take me for a decent walk. His mother bribes him to take me for a walk twice a day, in the park, because she feels he 'needs the exercise.' Looking at him I think she's right.

He goes round the corner all right, but once out of sight he either sits on a bench and plays with his phone or doubles back when he thinks his mother isn't looking. Then he hides me in the garage while he sneaks into the kitchen and takes a snack from the biscuit barrel. And he never gives *me* a biscuit. When I get given a biscuit it is in the shape of a bone. Who are they trying to kid? Are they trying to fool me into thinking it's a bone? A bone doesn't look like that – a bone doesn't *smell* like that. And, even worse, when he *does* give me a biscuit – er, bone – he expects me to turn into a circus act before he'll let me have it. Now if it was Thai green curry, for example, I'd sit down, beg, roll over – I'd do a cartwheel if I could – but it isn't. It's a boring bone-biscuit.

In fact, I know I should like Cyril, in a dog way, but I can't help worrying that he's going to do something nasty to me. He doesn't seem to realise that I'm not a toy and that I have feelings, like he does. I remember Mr Pearce talking about the Second World War and how the Russians trained their dogs to run suicide missions with mines strapped to their backs. I hope Cyril hasn't done the Second World War yet, because I think it might put ideas into his head.

He doesn't seem to have any friends, never talks to me and seems almost incapable of laughing. The only time I saw Cyril laugh was when he gave me some bubblegum and my teeth got stuck together. It was most humiliating, because I've had a lot of bubblegum in my time and I used to be able to blow the biggest bubbles in the whole school. But the new jaws I've been given don't work quite the same way. I thought it was mean of him to laugh like that. I don't think that strapping a mine onto my back can be too far away.

I'm on a long lead attached to the kennel. It looks like a washing line to me. So although I can get out of the kennel I can't exactly *go* anywhere. When the milkman comes I ask him to let me off.

'Excuse me,' I say very politely. 'Would you mind undoing this line? I don't think they meant to leave me tied up and they've gone somewhere in the car. I think they'd be very grateful if you did, because it's not very kind leaving me chained to a kennel. I'm not going to run away, because when you leave you'll be shutting the gate. I'm supposed to be guarding the house. It's difficult to do it properly from here. I need to *patrol* round it a bit.'

'Stop that crazy barking!' the milkman says as he leaves the bottles on the doorstep.

I have to watch the sparrows peck holes in the top and drink the milk and I can't do anything about it.

What rotten luck to have been the only girl in the litter. I bet the others have got really nice homes. I bet none of them sleep in a *kennel*. Anyway, kennels are so *old-fashioned* for a dog these days, unless you're a proper *working* dog. I wish I were a working dog. Then at least I'd have something to do.

My ears prick suddenly, all on their own. There is someone at the door of the house. Perhaps someone is going to play with me. I run out of the kennel like I'm fired out of a cannon, only to be choked by my collar when I reach the end of the cord. My legs sort of disappear from under me and I roll over and over. I get up quickly and shake myself. I don't want to look stupid. It wasn't for me, anyway. It was someone collecting for the Lifeboats. I'm tempted to do it again so that it looks as if I meant to do it all along, but there's no one there to see now, so I go back into the kennel. I feel embarrassed. It looked as if I hadn't worked out the four legs thing when in fact I was the first in our litter to go from crawling to standing up. Of course the others soon followed.

None of my brothers wanted to be outdone by a *girl*. It was my idea to bring the slipper back too, although they chewed it more than me. So I moved on to chair legs, which weren't as much fun but a real *challenge*.

I'm so bored now I wouldn't even mind if Cyril's mum did her training session. She has taken it upon herself to teach me how to *sit, stay* and *leave*! Well, it's perfectly obvious to me what *sit* means. She doesn't have to say it slowly, in a loud voice, as if I come from a foreign country. And I hate the way she wags her finger at me. Sometimes, just to be awkward, I pretend I don't know what she's talking about.

'No, Misty! I said SIT, not lie down.'

I also like eating the treat when she is holding it out in her hand asking me to LEAVE it. Why would I want to do that? Particularly when it looks as if she's giving it to me.

But the most fun I had was when she first put the lead on me and expected me to walk along at her side. Firstly she clearly doesn't understand that us dogs need to sniff at everything as we are

17

walking along. So I'd lie down and make her drag me along the pavement or, even better, go *backwards*. Still, even the most fun things get boring after a while, so now I just trot along at the end of the lead, grateful that I'm out of the kennel.

So here I am, out of the kennel. Cyril and I are at the bench again, he on his phone, me waiting for *someone* to throw me a ball. I have my head on my paws and now I'm watching some ants busying themselves in front of my nose, on the grass. They are moving a portion of a sweet and they are so organised. Part of a team. I miss being part of a team. If Miss Roberts, our games teacher at school, could see the way I run *now*, I'd be made captain of the football team.

I carry on watching the ants. There's nothing for *me* to organise any more and I wish there were. Other than move my bone around the kennel there's nothing to do. I used to have a book called a Personal Organiser and it had all sorts of stuff in it. I kept cinema tickets of films I'd liked, receipts for hot chocolate in the coffee shop and the ticket for the bus I was on when Owen Taylor was upstairs. But not now. Now there is nothing for me to file away, though I'm sure if I could get my hands on a few sheep, I could organise *them*.

Yes, there's a whole world down in that grass.

I see a group of boys swaggering towards us. I stand up to make myself look bigger. There's something about them I don't like.

One of them stops.

'What you up to, dude?' he says. 'Should you be out without your mummy?'

Cyril tries to hide his phone and shrinks back into the bench. I can feel the hairs bristle up on the back of my neck. This must be making me look at least twice my size by now. I feel big, anyway. It fills me with confidence. I don't think I'm scared, I just don't like them. I don't have to sniff them, I can already smell them and they smell of meanness and cowardice and boredom.

'Or is that your mummy?' they say, pointing at me and laughing.

Now I can take a joke at the best of times,

but this isn't even *funny*. I feel sorry for Cyril. I was bullied at school by a horrible girl called Jessica Warner. She and her gang of friends would poke fun at me and spread stupid rumours that weren't true. I growl at them. It's the first time I've tried growling properly and it makes me want to cough.

It's good not being afraid. If I were Cyril, I probably would be. But I'm here to protect him. After all, that is the deal. I give Cyril and his family devotion and loyalty and they feed me, walk me and love me back. Well, that is how it is supposed to work.

'I don't think you'll be needing that phone any more,' one of them says and steps towards us to take it. I growl again, louder. It's a strange, angry, *how dare you?* sort of noise that scrapes the back of my throat.

The boys back off and I add a snarl and bare my teeth for show. It is very effective.

An old man, who was sitting on another bench a little further along, gets up and walks towards us.

'You all right, son?' he asks Cyril.

Son? I think. This man doesn't look like Cyril's dad, unless Cyril's dad has gone out in disguise. For a start, he is much older and has shabby clothes on. Cyril's dad would not be seen dead without his suit on and one of his ghastly comedy ties.

No. This man is definitely not Cyril's dad.

'Clear off!' he says to the group of boys.

'All right, old man. Keep your hair on!' one of them shouts, and they pull their hoodies over their eyes, dig their hands deep into their pockets and stroll off, laughing. We all watch them go. I notice Cyril has sweat patches under his arms. I want to feel good about him, lick him to say it's OK, but I can't help thinking that if he'd taken me for a proper walk none of this would have happened.

'That's a fine-looking dog,' the old man says, ruffling my ears. I like that. Having my ears ruffled. I roll onto my back. I also like having my tummy tickled.

Well S-O-R-R-Y. But I do. It's a *dog* thing.

'What's her name?'

Cyril remains silent. He's probably still in shock

and I'm pretty sure that his mother has told him not to speak to strangers.

'Well go on, Cyril, tell him my name!' I say.

'Misty,' Cyril mutters, looking over his shoulder in case his mother can see him.

'Mr T? That's a funny name for a female.'

'MISTY. The dog's name is Misty.'

'Ah,' replies the old man.

He rests himself on the bench and we all sit in silence for a while. Then Cyril gets up and starts to drag me home. I don't want to go. I like this man. His face is weather-beaten and wrinkled and he has the bluest eyes. Besides, I think it's rude to go when he has just helped us out. Shouldn't we be inviting him back for a cup of tea?

'Thank you!' I say to him as Cyril yanks me away. 'For getting rid of those boys.'

It's the next day and we are back in the park. Cyril is looking anxiously around in case the boys are there again. Then he does something he has never done before. Instead of shutting me in the garage while he raids the biscuit barrel, he ties me to the park bench and goes back home. I sit there waiting for him to return. After all, I am a dog and loyalty is in my bones.

I check out the area. There is something lying on a bench further down the path. It is like a huge bundle of clothes. It moves a bit, stretches and sits up. It is the old man we met the day before. He has a few bags which he collects together and then slowly stands up, puts his hand on his back and rubs it.

When he sees me he walks towards me and I wag my tail like mad. I like this man. My tail feels as if it is attached to a motor. It goes round and round and I couldn't have stopped it if I wanted to.

'Hello, girl,' he says, rubbing my head like he did before. 'Have they left you here?'

He sits down on my bench.

'It's a fine day, isn't it? Why aren't you out on a nice long walk, eh?' he chuckles. 'It's a grand world out there, you don't want to be spending it tied to a bench.'

I totally agree with him. I want to tell him about

my circumstances, but just a funny little whimper comes out and takes me by surprise.

'I used to know a dog like you. He was a spirit dog. Dogs with two-coloured eyes are believed to be spirit dogs. They guide people. Don't go near a farm, mind. Farmers hate dogs like you. You'll freak the animals out. It's your eyes, see. No, you won't be popular if you go onto a farm. I bet you're a good companion, though.' He carries on. 'That boy shouldn't just leave you tied to a bench. It's not right. I'd take you with me if I could, old girl. But I don't want no trouble for stealing a dog. And it would be a hard life for you. I bet you've got a nice warm bed on some sofa somewhere.'

'No, I haven't! I live in *a dog kennel!* I'd love life on the road. I went on a walking holiday with Mum once and it was great!'

He nods sympathetically.

When he sees Cyril returning, the old man stops stroking my ears. He picks up his bags and shuffles off. He moves slowly, as if his feet cause him pain. I watch him as he goes down the path, his words jumping excitedly in my mind. A *spirit dog*. I like the sound of that.

And this is when I have The Plan.

Chapter 3

I spend most of my time lying in my kennel thinking about The Plan. Sometimes I'll think about The Plan with my eyes shut and sometimes I'll think about The Plan with my eyes open. But all the time I am thinking, planning and plotting. And sometimes I'm worrying about Mum and Dad. I hope Dad's hearing hasn't gone in the accident, because he loves music. He loves the Beatles, but he loves one type of music in particular: modern jazz.

When I was little he taught me the names of his favourite jazz musicians. I didn't know who any of them were, they were just names, but I remembered them for him because it seemed to make him happy.

I know it seems as if dogs sleep a lot. But it's a fact, in my experience, that there is a lot more going on. When a dog is truly asleep they dream. And when they dream it is of running through open fields filled with wild flowers, chasing rabbits or deer. You can see their paws twitching sometimes because in their dream they are running so fast they are almost flying.

But I'm not dreaming about that sort of thing. Maybe that sort of dream will come later. I am dreaming about home and Mum and Dad.

Once I dreamt I was at my funeral.

I was in a white coffin on a plinth and it wasn't in the local church, it was in a huge cathedral with enormous stained-glass windows. It was dark in the cathedral but the sun was streaming through the coloured glass like spotlights and fell onto the coffin. It was like being at the school disco. In this dream I started to dance in the coffin and the best thing about the dream was that I was dancing with Owen Taylor!

Although it was me in the coffin, I was also sitting in a pew, observing it all.

A small brown creature stepped into the aisle in front of me. At first I thought it was a fox. It had a long tail with a white tip to it. It trotted up the aisle and jumped into my coffin. And just before it jumped in, it turned and looked at the *me* who was sitting in the aisle. It wasn't a fox. It was *me* – as a dog.

The Plan is simple but it does need a lot of thought.

The Plan is to escape!

The Plan is to escape and find my dad and be his *spirit dog*! Like the old man said. I liked the idea of being a guide dog. After I'd got into trouble at Brownies for pulling silly faces at Brown Owl I hadn't been allowed to join the Girl Guides. Being a guide dog was going to be heaps better.

You don't have to be blind to have one. I'd seen people in wheelchairs with guide dogs. In fact, I'd watched a programme on the television about them. This particular dog – a Labrador, I think – could do ninety different tasks. *Ninety!* It could do things like take his master's wallet out and give it to the cashier in the shop. Fetch keys and other useful things. Go and get help if needed. Take the washing out of the tumble dryer. Well, *I* could do all those things. And I'd hang the washing up, as well. *And* I'd colour code it. And the best thing of all is that I could be back home again with Mum and Dad! Just like it used to be. Well – *almost.* Perhaps they've kept my old room just as it was and I can sleep on the bed. I don't think they'd be too strict about that. And I could go and fetch the paper in the morning and sit by Dad all day long and watch those black-and-white films he so enjoys.

Sometimes when I'm thinking about The Plan my tail will begin to wag. *Thump, thump* on the floor of my kennel. I am happy in my thoughts. And this is how I spend my time. Sometimes with my eyes shut. And sometimes with my eyes open.

Of course, it's all very well *making* A Plan. And it's all very well *thinking* about A Plan. But it's quite another matter making it happen.

Firstly – I have to escape.

Secondly – I have to find my way home.

And thirdly, I don't have the faintest idea where I am.

I reckon that my old home must be somewhere in the region – say within a radius of fifty miles. I know this because I read about my death in a newspaper. And only *local* newspapers would bother to make such a big thing of it. You know, the pictures and the captions and the reminiscences.

'She was such a lovely girl,' said a neighbour. 'Always very helpful. Especially with my post.'

Especially with my post! I only took a parcel for her once! Why couldn't she have said something about me being able to cycle past her gate with no hands on the handlebars at the same time as standing on the saddle of my bike?

'She was such a lovely girl. So acrobatic. Do you know, she would cycle past my gate, with no hands on the handlebars and standing up on the saddle of her bike? AND she helped me with my post.'

30

But even if I have to travel fifty miles I still have to escape.

Cyril has begun to make a habit of leaving me tied to the park bench. I suspect his mother has seen him leaving me in the garage. Really I just want someone to play with me. I'm spending too much of my time being tied up.

I keep a lookout for the old man. Sometimes I can see him across the park, looking in the rubbish bin, and sometimes he just appears, as if he's stepped out of thin air. Either way, my tail seems to notice him first and it wags and wags. It must be funny to be a dog without a tail. I suppose you have to just wiggle your bottom end.

He always comes and talks with me when Cyril's not there. He's told me how he used to have a dog when he was younger and how he misses the company now. But I want him to tell me if he has a family, and why he's sleeping in the park.

One day he's sitting on my bench as if he's waiting for me.

'Don't mind me,' he says to Cyril as we go past.

31

'I'll watch the dog for you if you like.'

But Cyril hurries on and leaves me at another bench.

'Over here!' I shout as soon as Cyril has gone. 'I'm behind the tree!'

The old man picks up his bags and ambles over. I notice that he's short of breath when he sits down.

'Well, old girl. I must be moving on. It's soon going to be too cold for sleeping in parks. I'll miss our little chats. Just wanted to say goodbye to you and wish you a good life.'

He fumbles in his pocket and produces half a mint. It has some fluff clinging to it and it is a bit smeared but it is delicious and it makes my breath smell of a sweet shop.

When Cyril comes back he tells me to stop whining and pulls me roughly by the lead.

But I am crying because I am thinking I won't see the old man again. I watched him leave the park and when he got to the gate he turned round and gave me a wave. I feel I've lost my only true friend.

After that, the park doesn't seem the same. I

notice the trees are dropping their leaves. Perhaps they are feeling as sad as me. I lie there and look up at the sky. It looks just like the jigsaws my aunt gave me for my birthdays that seemed to be nothing but sky, only none of the pieces are missing. I don't know where she got them from but there was always just one piece missing.

'Never mind, Daisy,' she'd say. 'Don't waste your time looking for the missing pieces. Just see the picture as a whole. I expect that missing bit is down the back of someone's sofa.'

I am lying down under the bench, wondering why people couldn't put their litter in a bin and wishing that the old man would come back, when I hear a dog barking somewhere in the park.

'Watch out!' it barks. 'Danger!'

I get up to have a better view and sure enough I see Danger strolling along the path with their hoodies pulled over their eyes and their hands dug deep into their pockets. It is the group of boys. They stop by the dog who was barking. He must be old, because I don't think he's tied to a bench, yet he's not running away. He's standing his ground and carries on barking at them. One of the boys looks as if he's going to run at the dog but instead takes a well-aimed kick. His boot hits the side of the dog and it rolls over and yelps. Part of me wants to go over and help, yet the other part of me feels scared of the boys and what they may do to me. I hear them laughing as the dog limps hurriedly away, licking itself. I think they're going to follow it and kick it again but then one of the boys sees me, tied to the bench, and points at me.

They start to walk towards me, pushing and jostling each other as if they are choosing which one will kick *me*. My paws begin to sweat and my heart is pounding in my chest. I'm not hanging around for that.

I try to run, but Cyril has tied some fancy knot he learnt at Scouts and the more I pull, the tighter my lead becomes. The boys are so close now I can smell what they've had for breakfast. I pull back on my haunches and flatten my ears tight against my head. The collar suddenly slips off over my nose and I am away. I don't stop to look behind me. I just run. I have never run so fast. There is no ball to chase, just open parkland, and as I run the wind catches my ears and they stream out behind me. I have left those boys a long way back. Full of relief, I bark with joy.

'I'm free! I'm free!'

And all the other dogs in the park, all those dogs in their collars and leads, answer me.

'Good luck!' they bark and I am through the park gates and out into the world.

I run past Cyril's road, behind the back of the school and out into open scrubland. I have never run so fast, nor so far. Miss Roberts would have been proud of me. As I run, birds on the ground fly up into the air and I shout at them just to scare them a bit more. I run through a patch of dandelions and my tail catches their seed heads and they float upwards in the breeze. I splash through a small stream and run through a wood. I have never felt so free.

I come to a halt on the outskirts of a suburb, my tongue hanging out and my whole body panting. It is getting dark. I still have no idea where I am and I am tired and hungry. I sniff the air. Some rabbits have been nearby but there's no sign of them now. I'd like to see a rabbit. Any sign of life would do right now. Not to eat. I'm OK about not eating at the moment, but I would like the company. I feel so lonely. The joy of running away and being free has left me. I miss Mum and Dad more than ever.

It's funny how little things can cheer you up though. I find a bush and clear out a bed from underneath. Round and round I turn. How good it feels not to be inside that kennel.

I keep on turning until finally I flop down and sleep. And I dream a proper dog dream. My legs would have been twitching. I run through the open fields but there are no wild flowers. And it is *me* who is being chased. Firstly by the group of boys and then by Cyril's mum. She is in the pink dress and she is yelling at me as she speeds across the ground.

'Come back at *once*, Misty! I paid good money for you!' But I keep on running and when I wake up I am as tired as when I went to sleep.

It is probably about six in the morning. I guess this because I can hear the song of the birds. I yawn and stretch out. I am thirsty as well as hungry. I wander out onto a patch of grass and lick the dew off it. I prick my ears. I can hear the rumble of a dustcart and the occasional lorry thundering along a road somewhere. I have to say, my hearing is fantastic now. There will be signs on that road, I think. Perhaps I'll recognise some of the names.

I trot off towards a small parade of shops. There is no one in sight and I have a good rummage through the bins that have been left out for collection.

Urgh, this is *disgusting*!

Fancy being reduced to this. Looking for other people's leftovers. I find some chips in a bag and a slice of stale bread. They don't smell too bad after all so I wolf them down. At the next bin there is half a McDonald's. Mum never let me eat junk food. It tastes good. What have I been missing all this time? I'm going to make a habit of going through bins in future.

The sound of traffic is getting louder now and there seem to be some signs of life. The newsagent opens his doors and a boy on a bike wheels up to collect his newspapers. I'm surprised how pleased I am to see him and I wag my tail. When he sees me, however, he pushes his bike towards me.

'Get off!' he says. 'Go away! Leave me alone!'

I remember that a lot of dogs like to frighten newspaper boys and postmen and for a moment – only a moment, mind – I can see the temptation to grab the bottom of his trousers and give them a little tug.

'It's OK,' I say. 'Why would I harm you? I'm just a bit hungry. You don't have a mint or something by any chance, do you?'

'What's all that wretched barking?' A man in an apron comes out of the shop and hands the boy a big bag of newspapers.

'Clear off!' he says to me. 'Wretched dogs! Always going through the litter and tipping it over the street.'

'Actually, I haven't done that,' I say. 'Sorry, though. Have *you* got a spare mint or anything?

Not bubblegum though, because it makes my jaws stick.'

'Clear off, I said. Stop that barking.'

And the man picks up an old Coke can lying on the pavement and throws it at me. I manage to dodge out of the way and I hear the can rattling along the gutter as I turn on my heels and run off, my tail between my legs. I try to move with purpose, as if I know perfectly well where I'm going. I don't, but you can't afford to idle if you're a dog on your own.

When I'm out of sight I slow down. There is a strong smell of cat. I can feel my heartbeat quicken. I see it, further along the road. It is a long-haired tabby and it is sitting, lazily washing its paws. I like cats. I like their independence. I like the feeling when they choose your lap, above all other laps, to sit on. Yes, I like cats. Normally. But this cat reminds me of Jessica Warner and how she would preen herself in front of the mirror in the school cloakroom. I hated Jessica Warner. She wore her school skirt upside down, with the elasticated waist six inches above her knee because it looked tighter that way. And she was forever flicking her hair from side to side.

I watch the cat get up and make eye contact. Then, before I can stop myself, I have this incredible urge to chase it along the street.

'I've got you, Jessica Warner!' I shout as I take off after her. 'Bet that's wiped that silly grin off your face!'

The cat runs across the road and I run after it. Too late I hear a whirring noise and a loud *clunk*. Then the sound of bottles smashing on the road. I didn't see the milk float. I dodge round a parked car and after the cat, which by now has run straight up a tree. It sits there, hissing at me.

'I've never liked you, Jessica Warner! You're mean, spreading those rumours about me. You shouldn't have said those things to Owen Taylor. I don't have a life-size cardboard cut-out of him in my bedroom. I hardly even *like* him and now he thinks I'm some sort of freak. And you look totally stupid with your skirt worn upside down. Hasn't anyone ever told you to tuck the label in?'

The cat turns on its tail and climbs higher up the tree.

'Ha! You'll be stuck up there until someone calls the fire brigade,' I shout.

I stand under the tree and continue shouting at her until a man comes out of a nearby house and throws a bucket of water over me. It's so mean I wouldn't be surprised if it is Jessica Warner's dad.

'Stop that blasted barking!' he shouts.

But I don't care. I shake myself violently, sending an arc of water into the air, which catches the morning sun and makes rainbow patterns all along the pavement.

I can hear the traffic quite well now but I'm having trouble finding it. All the roads look the same round here and most of them seem to be cul-de-sacs. Out of desperation I make what I think will be a short cut through someone's garden. As soon as I round the shed all hell breaks loose.

'Get out! Get out! This is *my* garden,' shouts a dog when he sees me. He is *huge*. He must be four times my size and has the most enormous fangs.

I'm backing off now.

'Look, I'm sorry, OK? I made a wrong turning.'

He takes a giant leap at me. His neck and his

jaws are absolutely massive and there's clearly no point in reasoning with him. He's backed me up against the dustbins and I've nowhere to run. He lands inches away from my nose, saliva dripping from his teeth. I don't know why he's not tearing me to pieces until I see that he is attached to a chain.

I see a hole in the broken-down brick wall at the end of the garden. I dodge round the heap of scrap metal and dash through the stinging nettles. I'm through the hole now and I look around. I'm in someone else's garden.

Compared to the yard I've just been in, this garden is like an oasis. I stand still and listen. I am listening for the sound of another dog. There are other dogs barking now, in the neighbourhood, but this house doesn't seem to have one. But what it does have are guinea pigs!

I love guinea pigs. I always wanted guinea pigs when I lived at home, but Mum would never let me have them.

'I'll end up having to look after them, Daisy, and I've got enough work as it is.'

I wasn't convinced by this. Mum wore a locket round her neck and she always fiddled with it when she was anxious or not sure of herself. I didn't think she was totally convinced about not wanting me to have guinea pigs because she was playing with her locket when she said it.

I go over and have a look at them. There is a ginger one and a tortoiseshell one and they are wrinkling their little noses at me, which makes their whiskers twitch, and making adorable little snuffling noises. I lie down to get on their level. I love guinea pigs, but not so much that I wouldn't mind *eating* one. I'm absolutely starving, and apart from looking fun to play with, they look rather *delicious*.

They scuttle back into their hutch. I can't reach them because they have a run made of chicken wire and it has a lid on it.

'Hey! Come back. I only want to *talk*,' I tell them.

The other dog must have woken the people who live here, because they are very quick to get to the window.

'Oi!' a woman shouts when she sees me. 'Leave them alone! Shoo!' She turns away slightly to talk to someone else in the room. 'Darling, there's a fox in the garden trying to eat your guinea pigs!'

A fox? This woman clearly needs glasses, but I'm not staying to tell her that. I dash round the side of the house and back into the cul-de-sac, practically knocking over the boy with the newspapers, who was just getting off his bike.

'Sorry!' I say as I take off up the street.

After a few more wrong turns I hit a ring road. By now it is full of lorries and cars. There is a complicated arrangement of signs telling you things you mustn't do. No stopping. No overtaking. No driving over 50 mph. I search for a route sign. There it is. Just after the sign telling you that tiredness can kill. Middleswick. Left at the roundabout. I knew it!

We spent a weekend at school doing orienteering and I was given the map. I knew just how to follow the roads. I even got two merits for leading my team from the crossroads at Middleswick back to the schoolground by way of the bus station.

The only trouble is – how to cross to the other side? Most of the vehicles don't seem to be obeying the sign telling them to travel no faster than 50 mph. I wait by the side of the road for a gap in the traffic and shout at them.

'Slow down! Can't you read? No faster than 50 mph. Are you blind or what? I'm trying to cross the road here!'

There is no point in following the Green Cross Code – you know, looking right, left and right again. I would have looked like one of those nodding dogs people have in the back of their cars. As it is I am beginning to feel dizzy. So I make a dash for it. I run into the road, dodging cars left and right. I see an open space and I make for it. A little patch of blue sunlight. I can hear the squeal of brakes. The sound of horns being blasted. I think I even hear the noise of bumper hitting bumper. But I just keep running and I am across, under the wire and into the fields on the other side. I am running towards Middleswick and Mum and Dad. Running towards my cool bedroom with the bed that was a mattress on the floor and the 'Save the Planet' posters and the pink mosquito net and the window overlooking the back garden.

I keep running for the rest of the day, across fields and through woods. I keep off the roads and, apart from some people on horses in the distance, I don't come across anyone. When night draws in, I make myself another bed in some long grass at the edge of a field and sleep a dreamless sleep.

I wake up to a bright light. At first I think it's morning. Then I see the light is coming from a truck, which is moving across the field towards me. It has three or four headlamps attached to the roof as well as the ones in the front, and it lights up the whole field. I can hear the murmur of men talking. I shrink back into the undergrowth. The light picks up a couple of dogs sniffing the ground. I think they may be bloodhounds. They are huge and have an awful lot of face about them. I wonder what they are doing out here. I feel sure that whatever the reason it's against the law. And I don't intend to hang around and find out.

I turn to sneak away, but the white tip of my

tail is caught in the beam.

'Fox!' cries one of the men. 'Let's get it for a laugh!'

What's with this fox stuff? I think. Can't they see I'm just *a dog*?

The bloodhounds pick up my scent and quicken their pace, barking from deep down inside their bellies. If I weren't so scared I'd be impressed by the noise they are making. I think my own bark hasn't properly broken yet. It sounds a bit small and high pitched. But I am terrified. Fancy being set upon by my own kind. Don't us dogs stick together?

The headlamps show only open fields with nowhere to run to, but I take off, the hounds close on my heels and the trundling truck not far behind. This is worse than that dream of being chased by Cyril's mum. I'm fast, but I think those other dogs probably have stamina. Something Miss Roberts always told me I didn't have.

I look around for a hole I can get into. Surely a real fox must have made a den somewhere? Or a badger? I'm not fussy. But there is nothing.

In spite of the fact I have been running all the previous day my legs just keep going. I don't even have to think about it. They just keep working while my head is busy thinking up something to do that will throw them off my track.

Suddenly, something rears up in front of me. I stop for a moment, wondering what it is. We both stare at each other in horror and disbelief. It is a young deer. She seems frozen to the spot and it looks as if her big brown eyes are going to fill up with tears. She looks past my shoulder, sees the other dogs and she's off. Jumping and bounding across the field in the opposite direction. I start to run the other way and the bloodhounds quickly change scents. With more barking they take off after her.

The men in the truck lose interest in me too, when they see the deer. I think this is what they've been after all along. But I don't stop running till I get to the outskirts of a wood. Then I flop down, my tongue hanging out and my whole body panting.

I hope it gets away, that poor deer. I can't bear to think of it being torn to pieces by those huge dogs. I don't think it would have been expecting death when it lay down to sleep in that patch of field. I know, because I hadn't either, and if that deer hadn't been there it would have been me.

It is late afternoon and I round the corner into Alexander Avenue. How many times have I come round that corner, swinging my bag after school or pedalling my bike or running breathless because I'm late for tea? I can't see our house because there is a huge lorry parked near the gate. I stop to get my breath and lick my paw. I have cut my pad on some flints as I went across the field and now I've stopped running it begins to hurt.

I limp along the pavement towards number twelve. There are two men carrying something out of a lorry into our house. Mum and Dad must have bought a new sofa. Though I don't think much of the colour. Perhaps they've lost their sense of style after my death. Never mind, it looks comfy enough and I'll enjoy curling up on those big soft cushions. But there is more. There are chairs and tables and toys! Heavens – they aren't having another baby, are they? To replace *me*? How could they? Surely they are a bit *old* to have more kids?

It is then that I see the sign. It is a big square sign stuck on a post in the garden. It says SOLD.

I sit on the pavement and stare at the letters. However hard I try to rearrange them in my mind to say something different – like a message to me – I can't. They've gone. Mum and Dad have gone and haven't left a single clue for me. No note. Not even a phone number.

I watch a woman coming out of the house and walk towards the lorry.

'Yes – that box is for the living room. I've put coloured stickers on each box so that you can tell. Yellow – living room; green is kitchen.'

She sees me by the gate and stops.

'Hello!' she says, bending down. 'Are you friendly?'

I lower my head and wag my tail.

'I used to live here,' I tell her. 'With Mum and Dad. But now they've gone. Have they left you a note for me or a forwarding address, by any chance?'

She strokes my head.

'You've got no collar on. I wonder who you belong to?'

'Mum and Dad,' I say.

She stops stroking me and goes back into the house. I think she's coming back with a piece of paper with their new address on but instead she has one of those bone-shaped biscuits in her hand.

'You poor thing. It doesn't look as if anyone cares for you.'

At that moment a small girl comes out of our house.

'Mum – are we having a new dog?'

The woman shakes her head.

''Fraid not, darling. Moss wouldn't like it now, would he? Two dogs are one too many in this house. Now run up and find your bedroom. It's the one with the window looking over the back garden.'

'That's my bedroom,' I say after I've eaten the biscuit. Mum always warned me about talking with my mouth full. 'Is there still a mattress on the floor and a pink mosquito net?'

But somehow I know there won't be.

'Now you'd better move on, before Moss sees you. He's a very jealous dog,' the woman says, and she has a word with the removal men, goes back into the house and shuts the door.

I lie down with my head on my paws. I want to cry but I can't. I see a lifetime stretch out in front of me, scavenging in dustbins. What is going to happen to me? As hard as I try there is nobody who understands me. Nobody who can comfort me and tell me it'll be all right.

All my hopes and disappointments and realisations of what I now am get stuck in the back of my throat.

Out comes an extraordinary noise. I lie by the gate and howl.

Chapter 4

It begins to get dark. The woman in the house draws the curtains. Hundreds and thousands of stars are twinkling in the galaxy. I try to see Orion's Belt. And it is there. Three bright stars in a row and then, surrounding the belt, four more bright stars which are supposed to be Orion's body. Orion was a hunter in Greek mythology. I wish now I'd concentrated more in humanities. When Mr Pearce was talking about it, Jake Harris was distracting me with his ruler.

And then I see another star. It is the brightest star in the night sky. It is my star. Sirius. The Dog

Star. Somehow, looking up at that bright light, I feel comforted. I imagine it is someone looking over me. And it fills me with hope.

The removal people have left. The lights in the house are turned off and I know it is time to move on. But now I don't know where to go. I decide to cross Middleswick and go down by the station. It is a place I was never allowed to go to as a child. It was considered rough and dangerous. But I am free now. I don't belong to anyone so I can do what I like. Besides, I'm curious. I want to know what it is about a place that makes it *unsuitable*.

A small van is parked at the back of the car park and someone is dishing out soup and bread rolls. There is a shuffling queue of people. They don't *look* dangerous. Just tired and hungry. Like me. I think I might be in with a chance of a bread roll. I am starving again. That little bone-shaped biscuit, although nice, has not filled the gap.

I creep up slowly towards the van. Before I ran away from Cyril I never crept anywhere. I would trot – my head held high, my tail up. Now my head is down and my tail clamped firmly between my legs. There is a warm smell coming from the wagon. It smells a bit like Mum's carrot and coriander soup. I lick my lips.

'I recognise you!' says a voice. 'You're that spirit dog.'

A rough hand strokes the top of my head and I look up. It is the old man from the park.

'What's happened to you?'

I'm so pleased to see him I forget my manners and jump up.

'I ran away. It was after what you said about spirit dogs and such, and I thought I'd try to find Mum and Dad and be their guide dog. My dad's paralysed, you know. I'm a girl, actually. Daisy Fellows.'

'People can be very careless with their animals, can't they? But old Jack'll make sure you're all right. You look cold and hungry. Come and sit with us.'

Well, yes, I think. It would be nice to go and sit with him but it's food and water I'm after. It's all very well being stroked and patted but my stomach's rumbling and I'm going to dry up like a prune unless I get a drink.

The old man shuffles over to some sleeping bags piled up in a disused doorway.

'Pip! Wake up! We've got a visitor!'

The tousled head of a boy, a little older than me, appears from the pile of sleeping bags. He has dark hair and a mouth that looks as if he is always smiling. He rubs his eyes, yawns and stretches out.

'What time is it? It's not morning, is it?'

I like the look of him and go over and put my nose by him. You can tell most things you want to know about someone when you give them a sniff. He smells warm and kind and funny and sad. I don't know why people bother with all that hand shaking and small talk. Why don't they just give each other a good sniff?

'Where'd you find him?' The boy sits up.

'Looking for something to eat by the soup wagon.'

'He must be hungry. He can have my bread

roll, and I've still got an apple core in my bag.'
Pip rummages in his bag and gives me the piece of
apple. Then he does the best thing in the world.
He takes a small plastic bowl and a bottle of water
out of his bag and offers me a drink.

'Hey! Have you seen his eyes? They're different
colours,' he says, watching me drink. 'He's a
lovely boy, aren't you?'

'I'm not a boy, actually,' I tell him in between
laps of the water. 'I'm a girl.'

'She's not a boy. She's a girl,' the old man says.
'I remember her from when I was sleeping rough
in some park or other. She had some sort of name
that made me think of the weather. But I can't for
the life of me remember what it was.'

Oh, *please* don't remember, I think to myself. I
really don't want to be lumbered with Misty for
the rest of my life.

'Does she belong to anyone?' Pip asks.

'Not by the looks of it. Not any more. She's got
no collar. No name tag. She can be yours now,
Pip. Everyone needs a companion sometimes.
Especially *you*, right now.'

The boy, Pip, ruffles my ears just how I like it and I creep nearer his side. He has very brown eyes. But I feel torn. I feel a loyalty to Jack. After all, he was kind to me in the park, and gave me the idea about escaping, and now *he's* giving me his bread roll to eat as well.

I go back to Jack's side.

'I think you should look after Pip, old girl. He's new to the streets and I'm an old hand at it. Go on, Pip – give her a name.'

'Now, let me think. Weather . . .'

Pip thinks for a while and then he begins to smile and it lights up his face like the morning sun.

'Ray! I'm going to call her RAY!'

I spend my first night as the dog, Ray, as close to Pip as I can get. I don't think anyone sleeps much. It is noisy. There is some shouting and some arguing.

'Don't take any notice of that, old girl,' says Jack, rolling up his trouser leg. 'They're always at each other. They drink so much they usually can't remember what they're arguing about. It always starts with the same thing though. Who owns the sleeping bag?'

But I'm not listening. Jack has wrapped newspaper all over his legs and tied them up with string. And some of the paper looks really old.

'You looking at my newspapers, girl? They keep Jack warm, see. It can turn nippy at night and these newspapers do the trick. Remember that, Pip.' He turns to the boy. 'Remember that, if you're still on the streets when it gets really cold.'

Still on the streets? No proper bed? Apart from those nights under the bushes, I've always had somewhere to sleep. And I hadn't been happy under those bushes. And I'm not sure I am going to be happy in the station car park either. But at least I have Pip. Jack has asked me to be Pip's dog and so I will. And I decide I'll be the best dog anyone's ever had. I will be loyal, obedient and protect him as best I can.

I want to ask Pip what he is doing in the station car park. Why he doesn't have a home to go to and where his mum and dad are. But I don't want to be a nuisance when we have only just met. So I lie still, one eye half open, just to make sure that Pip is going to be OK. It seems a very long night.

In the morning, Pip tells me we will go and look for food.

'You coming, Jack?' he says to the old man. But Jack shakes his head.

'Not feeling too good today, Pip. It's me chest. Damp socks, you know. You go. Take care, mind. Don't let them take that dog. And don't let them take you either.'

Pip grins, puts a knitted hat on and gives me a tug. He has made me a collar and lead out of some string and I trot happily along at his side. It's quiet in the car park now and the soup wagon has gone. I can hear Jack coughing as we leave through the gate.

It is still quite early and very few people are about. Out in the street, Pip goes through the dustbins, just as I had.

'Here we are, Ray. Here's some leftover chicken.'

I gratefully chew around the bone. I am impressed that he has fed me before himself.

'Thanks,' I say and wag my tail at him. 'Barbecued chicken's my favourite after spaghetti bolognaise and Thai green curry.'

Pip finds a discarded sandwich, some soft fruit and a half-empty can of Coke. He thirstily drinks from the can – only to spit it out seconds later.

'Aargh! Someone's stubbed a cigarette out in it. That's disgusting.'

I sympathise with him and continuc to nibblc on the chicken.

We move into the park and Pip goes to sit on the swings.

'You know, Ray,' he says, 'we've got to be careful. I've run away from foster parents and if I'm found they'll get me back or lock me up somewhere so's that I don't escape again.'

'Me too!' I tell him and he strokes the top of my head.

'My mum died, see. So I was taken into care. But it hasn't worked out properly and . . .' He bends down to whisper in my ear. 'I'll let you in on a little secret.'

I hold my breath. No one has told me a secret since Susan Maitland confided in me that her mum had won the lottery and was scared that people would ask her for money if they found out.

'I'm going to look for my dad! He doesn't know, and I've never met him. I'm not sure he even knows he *is* a dad. Apparently Mum met him at college when they were students and she moved away before she found out she was pregnant. She told me that she was so happy with me she couldn't see the point in trying to find him and tell him.'

I wag my tail and jump up at him, thrilled with the similarity of our story. Well, of course he hasn't died or become a dog. But we are both looking for our dads and neither of them know of our existence.

'My mum's dead,' he goes on, 'and she didn't tell me about my dad until just before she died. She gave me a picture of him.' Pip's hand digs into his pocket and produces an old black-and-white photograph of a young man who looks just like him. He shows it to me proudly.

'He looks nice,' I say encouragingly.

Other people begin to arrive in the playground and Pip decides we should move on. We walk back into town and Pip shows me the library.

'I like it in here,' Pip says as we walk up the steps. 'I go and read the newspapers and look through the telephone directories for my dad. His name hasn't come up yet.'

'You can't come in with that dog, young man,' says a voice behind the desk. 'Didn't you see the sign? Guide dogs only.'

'But I *am* a guide dog,' I say. 'Well, I will be when I find my dad.'

'Shhh!' the other voice continues. 'This is *a library!*'

Pip looks disappointed. I want to say he could go on in and I'll wait outside but he just says 'Sorry!' and takes me out. I think that's nice of him, not leaving me, and I give him a little lick to make up for it. He takes his hat and jacket off and we sit on the jacket at the bottom of the steps. I sit cheerfully at his side, watching. There's plenty to look at and it's warm, being in the sun. Pip seems quite happy just sitting there. I suppose he is making A Plan, like I did. I hope I'll be included in it, whatever it is.

I lie down and put my head on my paws. I shut my eyes. It is getting busy now and lots of people are walking past us. Suddenly I hear a clunking sound by my head. I get up with a start. Someone has tossed a fifty-pence piece into Pip's hat.

'That's because of you, Ray!' he says, taking the coin out of the hat. Then he changes his mind and puts it back again. 'Let's just stay here for a bit, eh? I feel we're lucky for each other.'

By the end of the morning there is three pounds fifty in Pip's hat. He buys me a bone from the market and two bacon sandwiches. It feels good, being with Pip.

When we get back to the car park Jack is pleased with his sandwich, though I notice he doesn't eat all of it. He coughs quite a lot and puts the remains in his pocket for later.

Apart from Jack, Pip doesn't seem to have any

friends either. What I like about him not having any friends is that he talks to *me*. He tells me he's come to Middleswick by train.

'When I ran away I knew they'd send the police or the social worker to find me so I thought I'd better get on a train. I just got on the first one that was leaving. It was exciting, really. I had to jump over the barriers and I only got on the train because someone had got their coat caught in the door and it hadn't locked properly. I had no idea what direction I was going in. I had to get off at Middleswick cos I didn't have a ticket and the guard was coming round. I had to hide in the toilet until the train stopped at the station. That's how I met Jack, in the car park. So I was lucky, wasn't I? I wouldn't have met you either!' He lays his head on my neck.

For the next few days our routine is the same. We find some food somewhere, go to the park and sit on the library steps. Often the best food is found at the market after the fruit and veg people have cleared away. There are some really quite nice things. Apples, peaches, only a little bruised. I wish Mum knew about waiting for the market to pack up. She always wanted to get there early to get the best.

I'm not giving up on finding Mum and Dad, even though I'm with Pip now. And if I do, I'll show Mum the market when they've closed down. See, that would all be part of being a guide dog. *Showing* her things. And if I do find Mum and Dad, and Pip doesn't find *his* dad, perhaps he can come and live with us.

There's so much I want to know about Pip. Has he ever been to Turkey? Did he have a girlfriend? Where did he go to school? But he hasn't told me these things yet and I can't get him to understand that I want to know.

I try staring at him very hard to project my thoughts into his. Like a sort of Mystic Meg. But he just laughs and strokes my neck.

'What *is* it, Ray? Are you hungry?'

Then one day the librarian comes out and asks us to move.

'You're putting people off coming into the

library,' she says. 'Why don't you go home?'

'We don't have a home,' I snap at her. 'Isn't that *obvious*?'

But Pip just says, 'Sorry,' and we get up and leave.

We walk along the pavement. There is a family in front of us with a woman pushing a pram with a wailing child.

'Jodie!' she shouts. 'Where are you?' Someone pushes past us – a girl about my age – and there is something familiar about her. I look at her. She's eating an ice cream and it's dribbling down onto her pretty dress. It's the dress that looks familiar, I realise. It's turquoise with pink flowers on it. Then I realise it's *my* dress she's wearing! It couldn't have been anyone else's because my auntie had made it for me and I chose the fabric with her. What is this girl doing in my dress? And then I remember the Oxfam shop and how when my grandfather died, Mum sorted out his clothes and took them to the shop. I remember wondering what she would think if she saw someone wearing her dad's suit or nice Fair-Isle-knit jumper that

Grandma had knitted for him. And now here was a girl wearing my dress! Mum must have taken *my* things to the Oxfam shop too. How many other girls are walking around in my clothes? I wonder. Who's got my new skinny jeans that I'd only had for a couple of weeks? And my fake Abercrombie and Fitch hoodie I bought in Turkey?

I want to go and say something to her but Pip is crossing the road and I don't want to lose him. I am wondering now what they buried me in. I hope it wasn't the bridesmaid dress I wore at my cousin's wedding. That was ghastly and made me look completely childish. It had puffy sleeves and a full skirt. They told me I'd be able to wear it as my prom dress if I let the hem down. Honestly, everybody at school would have laughed at me if I'd turned up in that. I'd like to have been buried in my new coat with the fake-fur collar and, under that, the beautiful long, sea-green dress with the thin straps I'd seen when I was out shopping with Mum.

When we get back to the station car park Jack hasn't moved from his usual spot. His feet are sticking out from underneath his makeshift sleeping bag as if they can't bear to be contained and had to make a break for freedom. I go over and lick his face. He seems hot in spite of the fact the weather has turned and is getting colder. His clothes are damp too.

'He's not well, Pip,' I say. 'Can't we get him to the hospital or something?'

Pip kneels down at his side.

'Jack! Are you all right?'

But Jack doesn't stir. His breath is rasping.

'Come on, Ray. We'll have to find a chemist and get him something.'

I wag my tail. Good idea, I think.

We leave Jack where he is and go back into town. We find a supermarket that has a chemist in it and Pip leaves me tied up outside.

'You're not allowed in the shop, Ray. So you'll have to stay here. If anything happens to me you must get out of here. If anyone thinks you're with me they may put you in the dog wagon. Maybe go back to the station car park if you can find it. Do you understand?'

I wag my tail at him again. It seems the best way to show my agreement. But what on earth is going to happen to him, I want to know? As far as I can see he is going to get something that will help Jack get better and we will give it to him and everything will be all right.

'Good luck!' I say. 'Take care!' I'm beginning to feel uneasy about the whole thing. Pip goes into the shop and I sit down and wait for him.

It is just like having to wait for Mum when *she* went shopping. 'I'm just going to nip into the shop, Daisy, I won't be two secs!'

A million, squillion secs later she'd be hurrying back to the car.

'Sorry, darling – there was such a *queue!* And then I couldn't decide whether to buy the brown one or the green one. So I bought both!'

After a while Pip runs back out of the shop.

'Quick, Ray,' he says and bends down and unties me. But just as he does so a man and a woman come up behind him. They are wearing uniforms, but I don't think they are the police. For a start the man has a grubby mark on his jacket where he dropped something he was eating. I am sure that policemen aren't allowed to have grubby marks on their uniform. They are probably not even allowed to *eat* in their uniforms. I suddenly have an image of a lot of policemen eating their sandwiches in their helmets and underpants.

'We have reason to believe that you have taken something that does not belong to you. Without *paying* for it. Would you please empty out your pockets, sir?'

Pip does as he is told and takes out a box of pills from his jacket.

I look at him. I can see for a moment, in his eyes, the temptation to make a dash for it. But the man has a firm grip on his arm.

'They're for a friend. He's very ill. I wanted to give them to him,' says Pip, with a look of *Help me out here, Ray*, to me. So I chip in.

'Look. Pip is not a thief. It's just that we haven't any money and Jack is ill. It's his damp socks, you see. He's got some sort of chest infection and the pills are supposed to make him better. Though personally, I thought we should have got him to hospital.'

'This your dog?' says the woman. 'It's not got a proper collar and disc on.'

Pip looks at me sadly.

'No!' he says. 'I don't know who it belongs to.'

'Looks like a customer for the dog pound then,' the man says, taking his mobile phone out of his pocket.

A small crowd of people have gathered around like they're watching a piece of street theatre. A modern-day Punch and Judy show. I just need the string of sausages to make the tableau complete.

I remember what Pip said about getting out of here and as his eyes widen I know I have to make a dash for it. And I do. As I race for the corner, I can see the couple leading Pip back into the shop. The small crowd is still there. I want to go back and help him. Perhaps go for the man's throat or bite the woman's calves. I know this is sheer bravado and also that hanging around with a bit of string round my neck is not a good option. So I keep on running. But it isn't the joyous run I first made in the park, when I escaped from Cyril. It is more like the dream. And I run blindly, scattering people as I charge along the pavement. And my mouth is dry and my tongue is hanging out and I can feel saliva gathering in the corner of my mouth.

'What's up with that dog?' I hear someone say.

'It's probably got rabies. Did you see its eyes?'

'Rabies!' someone else screams.

Rabies? I think. Oh, how ridiculous! Where was I going to get rabies from, unless I'd been smuggled in from the Continent? I'd only been on that holiday to Turkey and a school trip to Bordeaux and that was – in a different life!

But by now there are a stream of people chasing me along the pavement. My heart is racing even faster than my legs. If only Pip were with me. If only I had wings like that chap who flew too near the sun. I try to think of his name as I tear across the square. But all I can remember is staring out of the window during the humanities lesson and watching Owen Taylor play football. I was sure he had winked at me and took no notice of Mr Pearce droning on about the dangers of the sun. Then I realised that Owen Taylor had just got some mud in his eye.

'He should have been wearing a factor-thirty sun cream, shouldn't he, sir?' said Jessica Warner to a giggling class. 'Look, sir. Daisy Fellows has gone bright red. Perhaps *she's* got too close to the sun!'

It's because of all this thinking that I don't see the bicycle. It shouldn't be on the pavement anyway. It's dangerous cycling on the pavement and can cause an accident. Which is exactly what happens.

As I race past, my piece of trailing string gets caught up in the pedals. The bike and the man riding it topple over and we all go crashing to the ground.

Then I suddenly remember. 'Icarus!' I say. 'Icarus! Icarus!' I'm sure it must sound as if I'm swearing blue murder as I fall.

Another crowd of people gathers around. Perhaps not as many as had probably collected by our car when it crashed. But still, quite a sizeable crowd. More than had been outside the supermarket.

'Is the dog all right?' an elderly woman asks.

'Damn the dog,' says the man, crawling out from underneath the bicycle. 'Doesn't matter about the dog! What about me? I've hurt my ankle and I've got a tear in my trousers!'

'You shouldn't have been riding on the pavement, mate!' someone shouts out.

'Yes! That's just what I was thinking,' I say. 'What do you think the road's for?' I begin to sound like my dad so I shut up.

'Oh, you poor thing,' says another person, detangling the string and stroking my head. I look wildly around me to see if the Rabies People are there, but they must have given up a few blocks back.

'Does this dog belong to anyone?' comes a stern voice. A voice of authority. The kind of voice that wears a uniform. And I am right! A policeman walks up to the scene. He *definitely* doesn't have any dinner stains on his uniform and I can see my face in the shine on his boots as approaches me. 'And what were you doing riding on the pavement, sir?'

We all murmur in agreement.

'What do you think the road's for?'

The policeman gets out his walkie-talkie. 'Right!' he continues. 'So no one owns the dog?'

A few people shake their heads. There is a lot of crackling coming from his handset and, holding my string firmly, he walks to the corner shop to get better reception.

I know what he is doing. He is ringing the dog pound.

Chapter 5

My kennel cell is between Max, a bull terrier, and Toby, a crossbreed.

Neither of them say much. In fact, neither of them say *anything* and I only find out their names because one of the wardens is showing two people around.

'This is Max,' she says, stopping outside his door. 'Max is worried by strangers and loud noises. He'd prefer a quieter life and could live with children, provided they're not very young. Do you have children?'

The couple look doubtful and then suddenly

remember that indeed they do have *two very young children.*

'Now this is Toby,' she goes on, ignoring me completely. 'Toby is a misunderstood dog who does not cope well with stress. He would like to relax in a home where little is expected of him. But he does like running through the tunnels and over the jumps.'

Golly, what tunnels? I think. Sounds fun – a bit like gym. As long as there's no rope climbing. For some reason I've never been good at climbing ropes.

'Come along, Daisy!' Miss Roberts would cry. 'Think *monkey!*'

Perhaps that's what they'll say when it comes to my turn. 'This is Ray. She hasn't been with us long so we don't know much about her, but she's absolutely hopeless at climbing ropes.'

'What about this dog with the funny eyes?' one of them asks.

'Ah. We can't tell you much about her. She hasn't been with us very long. She's awaiting assessment.'

They nod at me.

'Well, I can tell you all about me if you want,' I say, jumping up at the bars to get their attention. 'I like playing football, riding a bicycle, going to the cinema and baking cakes. I expect I would like running through the tunnels and over the jumps too. I'm not at all worried by strangers – in fact, my mum always said I was good with people.'

'She barks too much,' the woman says. 'It would not be good for the *children*.'

I sigh and lie down on my cushion. I look around me.

'How long have you been here?' I ask Max. 'Who were you, before you were a dog?'

But Max just stares at me and goes back to his corner. I remember that Max is worried by strangers so think I'll talk to Toby, but he is chewing on a bone so I decide not to disturb him. Really, where is the *communication*? It strikes me how silent the place is. No one seems to have anything to say. It is as if they've had their personalities sucked out of them.

I am thinking about having your personality sucked out of you and the fact that I went through the wrong door. The woman in the Job Centre had twice told me to go through the door on *the right*. And I had gone through the door on *the left*. Perhaps the door on the left had been a prototype and because of all the cutbacks they hadn't been able to afford to put a lock on it. Really! What if you couldn't read? They should at least have put a chain across it.

And now, suddenly, I know why I was supposed to go through the right-hand door. You're not supposed to remember who you've been in a previous life! Max and Toby, well, they must have gone through the door on the right and had their memories erased. I don't want to lose my memory. Getting my left and my right muddled up had been an advantage to me this time. If I forgot everything about me I wouldn't be me. I want to still be me.

I sit in the quiet space. Only the sound of the warden's voice drifts over the silence.

'Now George here loves a cuppa and a play

with his squeaky toy, but cats and small furry animals are a no-no.'

The dog pound is situated near a farm in the middle of nowhere. There is a fenced-off area, surrounded by fields, where we are taken to '*do our business*'. Those fields look so inviting that I long to stretch my legs and run through the grass. I stand by the wire fence and stare into the distance, wondering what has happened to Pip. And when I'm in my kennel cell I sit in my corner and wonder what has happened to Pip. And then the wondering turns to worrying. I imagine him locked in a police cell or back with his foster parents. Although I've only just met Pip I feel very close to him. I think it was the photograph that sealed our friendship.

And when I'm not worrying about Pip I worry about Jack. He is probably dead now, without those pills Pip took. And all because of his damp socks. Mum always went on about damp clothes and not going to bed with wet hair. 'You'll get pneumonia!' she'd say.

I never used to worry. Well, I suppose I worried the first day at school in case no one liked me, and I worried when it came to exams in case, after they said, 'Now turn over your papers,' I couldn't answer anything other than what my name was. So I wouldn't say I was the worrying sort. As a dog, though! The responsibilities of being a dog are *enormous*. You have to make sure your owner is safe. You have to make sure that no one burgles the house when they're out. And that can mean being worried *all day*. At the moment I'm worried that Cyril and his mum might come to the dog pound looking for me, even though I must be miles away from them right now.

My kennel cell is near the front desk. This means that I know of all the comings and goings to do with the pound. I can watch the girl who sits on reception eating sweets when she thinks no one is looking and using the phone to make personal calls. There is another girl who sits there sometimes who likes to do her nails.

I have learnt that all us dogs have a card with our particulars on it, pinned to a board by the front desk, and our fate is dictated by which way the card is facing. I know this because a nice man in a hat, who was doing volunteer work, was brushing one of the dogs up by the front desk.

'That's Bertie, isn't it?' said the girl at the desk, and she took his card down and turned it around.

'Why are you doing that?' the man asked.

'Bertie's got to go. I meant to turn his card around this morning. No one wants him and he snapped at one of the kennel maids yesterday.'

'Where's he going?'

'He's in for the chop!'

'Oh no he's not!' said the man, grabbing the card and tearing it up. 'He's coming with me. I'm not letting him be put down. Come on, Bertie! We're going home!'

The girl at the desk and I looked on in amazement as the man opened the door and took Bertie over to his car.

'Well I never!' I heard the girl say. 'Whatever next!'

The words 'in for the chop' rolled around my mind for the rest of the day. So that's what happens when a dog gets taken to that little room at the end of the corridor. I had noticed that they never come back. I only hope that it is quick.

The staff refer to these dogs that no one wants as 'sticky' dogs. Dogs that stick around. Max and Toby are definitely sticky dogs and I wonder if either of them take any notice of the cards and which way they face. I find I am constantly checking on mine now. So far no one has been interested in taking me. I must learn to keep quiet, I suppose. Actually, if I'm honest I haven't wanted anyone to take me, so perhaps I'll go on telling them what's what. Though I wouldn't have minded if the nice man in the hat had come back for me.

But really it's Pip I want to come in through the door and claim me back. Though I don't think they'd let Pip take me. They do all sorts of checks and go and visit the homes of the interested owners. They wouldn't be too impressed with a pile of cardboard and some old sleeping bags. I could tell them different, though. That it's not where you are but who you're with. And that in my opinion, Pip takes better care of me than Cyril and his family ever did. The dog warden people *would* probably be impressed with a pink furry loo-seat cover. But what do they know? They think dogs are dogs. But I know otherwise.

Max is the first to go.

They give him a biscuit and a pat on the head and lead him off to the little room. I hope with all my might that he believes he is going to a quieter life. And in many ways I suppose he is. I wonder if this is the end of the line for Max. Is he still a soul? Will he be in the Job Centre by now? Certainly, unlike me, he seemed to have no recollection of who he'd been in the life before. But presumably when he gets there he'll still remember being Max. Perhaps, with time, even though I went through the wrong door, I'll forget too.

I go over some things to remember in my head. Henry VIII's six wives, for a start. Their names and what happened to them. Divorced, beheaded, died. Divorced, beheaded, survived. I can't remember, though, if Jane Seymour was beheaded or just died, but I don't think that matters. I can still remember our telephone number and the registration number of Dad's car.

It's a few days later and I come back from '*doing my business*' and find that my kennel cell has been scrubbed out and I have been put on the other side of Toby, next to a blank wall. Does this mean the end for me? My card is still facing the same way but I remember Mum telling me that in some hospital wards the patients that weren't going to last the night were moved to the end of the ward. They'd done this with Grandad. The day before he died they put him at the end, near the exit door. He had a wall on one side and an empty bed on the other. There was a picture on the wall of a boat, battling through the waves. It was probably the last thing he saw before he died. Well, I hope so. You wouldn't want your last view to be someone emptying out a bedpan.

I am thinking about my grandfather and I hear a faint voice at reception.

'We're looking for a dog for my husband. A dog that would be a good companion and who could be trained to do simple things.'

My ears suddenly prick up.

'What sort of simple things?' asks the girl at the desk.

'Oh, like taking a wallet out of a pocket, for instance.' The woman clears her throat.

At first I think they must be pickpockets and that this is a novel idea, getting a dog to do it. But when she speaks again I know who it is. It is Mum! We watched the programme about guide dogs together!

Some chattering goes on that I can't hear, probably some form filling, and then, coming into sight, is Mum pushing my dad in a wheelchair. I practically turn a somersault I am so excited. It is like a prayer has been answered. There is Mum, looking a bit thinner and tired, but still Mum. She's cut her hair shorter, but I don't mind. And there is Dad, sitting upright in his chair, as she pushes him along the corridor. Since the accident he's grown a beard and his hair is flecked with grey. He has a look on his face that tells me that this idea of looking for a guide dog was definitely not his. I am excited and sad at the same time.

Dad will need a lot of looking after, I can see, but I'll be proud to do it.

'This is Ben. He likes splashing in puddles but probably wouldn't be very good at fetching things.'

'Mum! Dad!' I cry. 'It's me! Daisy! I'm over here! Look in my kennel. I've been trying to find you but you've moved homes. I don't mind really – it would be fun to live in a new house, and you've probably got lifts and hoists and things in it.'

'Gosh, that dog makes a lot of noise, doesn't it?' says Mum. She bends down to look at Ben. '*He's* rather sweet. Darling, what about this fellow?'

'No! You can't take *him!* I can do all the things other dogs can do and more.' I hesitate for a moment, remembering Jessica Warner, and not wanting to show off too much. 'Cats and small animals are probably a no-no, but other than that, take me! Take me!' I jump up and down at the railings, managing to tip my water bowl over at the same time.

'I'm sorry about all the noise,' says the warden. 'This dog hasn't been here very long. I don't know what's got into her. She's normally as quiet as a mouse.'

I don't believe in omens, but this morning a bird flew, smack, into the window. The window was too high to see what happened to it, but it hit with such force that I don't imagine it survived.

I watch Mum push Dad up to my door. She stops and peers at me.

'Oh, *you're* a sweetie,' she says and bends down to get a closer look.

I feel as if my heart is bursting out of my chest and I leap up at the door.

'Yes, Mum – it's your daughter. You can take me home now. I'll be so good. I know I won't have a bedroom to keep tidy, but I won't leave any bones lying around and I promise not to chew any slippers and I won't dig holes in the garden and I'll come when you call me and –'

'Look, Dennis. This little dog is so full of energy. Why don't we take *her*? There's something about her I like. I'm sure we can stop all the barking – she must be fed up being cooped up in here. I wonder what her story is?'

'She was probably abandoned *because* of all that barking,' my dad says.

My father and I look at each other and all the colour drains out of his face, like he's been a bottle that someone has suddenly tipped upside down.

'No! No! I couldn't live with this dog. Its eyes. It would just remind me of Daisy. It's hard enough as it is without thinking of her every time I look at it.'

'But, Dad – it *is* me.'

In desperation I roll over onto my back, trying to make myself as appealing as possible. Then when that doesn't seem to work I get up and try to lick his hand through the bars.

'Dad! Dad! I keep telling you, it's *me*! I'd comfort you. I'd always be around and I wouldn't argue much. You've got to change your mind and take me with you. I'll never complain or judge you or be embarrassed by your jokes.'

'Let's go,' my father says. 'Perhaps a dog isn't a good idea after all.'

As Mum turns the wheelchair around I try again.

'Take me. *Please* take me. Don't leave me here. I didn't mean to break those photo frames by your bed. It was an accident. The blanket got caught up when I was bouncing. I'm really, really sorry. I won't do it again.'

'Does that dog ever stop making a noise?' I hear Mum say. This is definitely my mother. She was *always* telling me I was making too much noise.

'Daisy – turn that thing down!'

'I imagine it would be difficult to find a home for a dog like that,' she goes on. 'It's a shame, because she looks such a sweet little thing.' She puts her hand to her neck and pulls out her locket, twisting it round her finger.

The warden nods in agreement.

'I can give you the number of Dogs for the Disabled if you like.'

And I watch them go back down the corridor. Dad's wheelchair makes a funny little noise like some small creature is stuck to the wheel and is making a squeal every time it hits the floor. I can hardly believe I've seen them and now I can't believe they've gone. I can't believe they've turned around and disappeared, leaving me here. All on my own. How can they not know it's me?

'Please don't go. I'm trapped in this body of fur, your daughter, who you always said you loved. If you leave me here you'll never see me again. I know you don't know it but I came looking for you and you never left a forwarding address. Why don't you look back? Why don't you see me?'

I strain my ears till I can't hear the squeaking any more and then I lie down on my cushion and I'm howling again. For my lost childhood and the girl I was and my lovely mum and dad. For the lost opportunity that I know won't happen again. For the grief I know they are going through. I want to tell them it is all right and that I'll always be with them. There are no tears running down my face to comfort me. I just have a huge pain in my chest, as if someone's ripped my heart out and stuffed the hole up with old newspapers.

They've left the building now and in the distance I can hear their car drive away.

As I said, I don't believe in omens, but the morning of our crash a young blackbird flew out of the porch straight under Mum's foot as she was walking in. It broke its neck.

It is later that day I notice my card has been turned the other way.

Chapter 6

All the dogs are let out at a regular time and, today, I am allowed out to the back field with them. The wardens always stand around and chat, drink a cup of coffee and smoke a cigarette, while we mind our own business.

I am sitting by the fence, wondering what will happen to me. I'm not afraid. Perhaps I'll get a proper job next time round – a *qualified* one. I wonder how far back I'll remember. For instance, if I went out of the wrong door again, and if I came back as, say, a human, would I remember being a dog? And would I remember being Daisy as well as being a dog? When I was Daisy I couldn't remember being anyone else. I think about Henry VIII's wives again, but am no clearer as to what happened to Jane Seymour. Hey – perhaps I *was* Jane Seymour in a previous life!

I am just imagining being Jane Seymour when I notice a spire of smoke rising from the dog pound.

'Fire!' someone shouts. The wardens rush into the building and I carry on thinking about Jane. There is quite a lot of smoke now, which sets off the fire alarm. Some of the dogs are barking. Through the mayhem I hear a voice.

'Ray!' it says. 'Ray! Over here. Quick!'

I look towards where the voice is coming from and there, right by the fence, is Pip. My heart almost leaps out of my fur.

'Pip!' I shout. 'You're all right! How did you get here? How's Jack? What's going on?'

'Shhhh, Ray,' he says. 'Don't make so much noise, they'll hear us.'

I see that he has cut a hole in the fence and that he is holding open the wires.

'What about the others?' I ask. 'Perhaps they'd like to get out too.'

I look back at the other dogs. There is Toby, sniffing around, and George, busy with his squeaky toy. I don't think Toby would be able to cope with the stress and none of the others seem interested. I squeeze through the wire and give Pip a big lick.

'Let's get out of here before they catch us. I set fire to some newspaper and put it in one of the dustbins to create a diversion.'

'What a brilliant idea!' I congratulate him and give him another lick. Then I run round him in small circles, telling him all the things that have happened since we parted outside the supermarket.

'Be *quiet*, Ray, they'll hear us. Oh no! They have! Let's go!'

I glance behind me and see one of the wardens making her way towards the hole in the fence.

'Oi! Come back with that dog!' she shouts. But we start to run. We run through the long meadow grass, scattering wild-flower petals as we go. Poppy, corn cockle, oxeye daisy. I know them all thanks to Mum and her love of flowers. It must look like a wedding with all this coloured confetti.

We cross one field and into the next. The skylarks are singing for a beautiful day. If Pip had thrown me a stick I would have fetched it. I definitely wouldn't have fetched a stick for Owen Taylor. And as we round the corner we come across some cows.

I'm not sure if they are Guernsey or Friesian. I wrack my brain for the right page in the *I Spy Book of Farm Animals*. I think you get twenty points for a black-and-white cow. Whatever their breed is, they are all looking at us and have herded together into quite a tight-knit group.

We stop running. I am standing by Pip. Well, I'm standing *behind* Pip.

I feel all the hairs on the back of my neck stand up in fright. Mum and I were chased by a bull when I was little and I can still remember flying along at the end of her hand as she raced for the gate. She wore a floral dress, like the meadow we have just run through, and for some reason I had on a woollen hat and leggings. I must have boiled.

Pip stands his ground.

'What shall we do?' I ask.

'Don't bark, Ray. You'll make it worse.'

The front line of cows lower their heads and start to come towards us. They have pretty big horns.

We begin to back off a bit. I am all for running away but Pip stands his ground and I love him for it. I love him more than Owen Taylor.

'Shoo!' he says and waves his arms. 'Get away with you!'

They are quite near us when they stop. They seem to be looking at me. I think we all must have been holding our breath. Then they snort in unison, shake their heads, turn tail and gallop off. I am quite surprised and then I remember what Jack had said to me when we met in the park. About my eyes freaking out farm animals.

'Come on, Ray, let's run for the other field before they change their minds and come back,' says Pip.

We turn to go. At that moment I would have run anywhere with him. But running towards *us* are two of the wardens from the dog pound.

'Come back here AT ONCE! That dog is not your property!'

'I AM!' I shout back at them. 'I belong to Pip. You can't take me back now. Besides, you turned my card around so you didn't want me anyway.'

And with that we run after the cows, leaving the wardens far behind. And the faster we run, the more crazy the cows go, until they are bucking and snorting and mud is flying in the air and I am laughing and laughing.

'It's *you*, Ray!' Pip pants. 'There's something about you that's winding them up! Ha! Ha! You *clever* dog!'

I like that. Pip calling me clever.

We are laughing so much I don't think either of us see the Land Rover with the farmer in it. He pulls up sharp and gets out. He is holding a shotgun.

'What do you think you're doing on my land?' he shouts, waving the gun at us. 'I've a good mind to shoot that dog. And I'm perfectly within my rights to do it. Not only are you *trespassing* but you've frightened my cattle. They're all in calf and this stupid behaviour will probably make them all miscarry. Do you realise how many hundreds of pounds that will cost me? Why can't you people stick to the footpaths?'

I'm sure I'm not alone in feeling sick to my stomach.

'I'm sorry, sir,' says Pip. 'We didn't mean it. We – I mean, I – wasn't thinking straight. I didn't see a sign for a footpath.'

'Are you calling me a liar? I have to put up a sign for you wretched people. Footpaths? Bah! Troops of townies walking over my property! Footpaths should be abolished.'

The farmer turns back to his Land Rover and goes to take something out. I am sure it is going to be extra bullets. He seems very cross. He produces a piece of paper.

'What's your name?' he says, taking a pencil stub out of his pocket.

'Er – Phillip. Phillip Seagrove.'

'And what's your address, Phillip Seagrove?'

Pip reels off a number and some street.

'I'll be sending the vet's bill to your parents then. And you've got five minutes to get off my land or I'll call the police. And as everything that you can see is my land, you'd better get going. And KEEP AWAY FROM MY COWS.'

The farmer reverses his Land Rover and tears off after the disappearing herd. I sit down on the grass and shake. Mum had a miscarriage when I was eight. I was going to have a baby brother and Mum and Dad were so excited. They decorated the spare bedroom and bought baby things and talked endlessly about what they would call him. I hated it. And I hated the idea of someone else in the family. I'd have to share my toys with him and later I'd have to babysit for him and I wouldn't have Mum and Dad to myself any more and wasn't I good enough for them?

And then Mum lost the baby. She had this miscarriage. She went to hospital and when she came back she cried and cried and they gave all the baby things away and turned the baby's room into a study for Dad. Though he never studied anything. And it was my fault. Because if I hadn't hated the baby so much it wouldn't have died. And now all those cows are going to lose *their* babies and that is all my fault too.

'Come on, Ray. We'll have to get out of here.'

But I won't budge. I feel too depressed. And I think that spirit-dog thing is probably a load of nonsense. I don't think those cows ran away from me because I have different-coloured eyes. I think they ran away from me just because I'm a *dog*.

'Ray! Come *on*! We don't want them to take you back to the dog pound do we?'

I kind of want to shake my head but the shaking-the-head muscles only seem to work if something is irritating it. Like an insect. Of course I don't want to go back to the dog pound. I want to be with Pip. I'll do anything for him. Anything he asks. Besides, I don't want to stay in the farmer's field. I think he's probably mad and will return with his shotgun loaded.

I struggle to my feet. I have burrs stuck to my fur.

'Is your name really Phillip Seagrove?' I ask.

'Come on, Ray,' he says. 'We need to get out of here.'

We are walking along the street now and it is getting dark. The soup wagon is back in the station car park.

'I'm starving, Ray. Bet you are too. Let's get some bread rolls and go and see Jack.'

'Jack?' My ears prick up. I like the way I can get them to change shape. I can make them pointed, floppy or flat. I can raise one ear independently of the other and I can make them fly when I run into the wind.

'Is Jack all right then? I've been worried. What about his damp socks?'

And there he is. Sitting on a piece of cardboard, wrapped in a sleeping bag.

'Ah, you're back, Master Pip, and you've got Ray. Well done, boy! Did that trick with the newspaper I told you about work?'

Pip nods his head. So it wasn't his idea after all.

But I still love him, nevertheless. I love the way he grins at me and strokes my head. I love his hair that flops in his eyes and makes him look like a rock star and I love the fact that he – well – seems to love *me*. Apart from Mum and Dad, I don't think anyone else ever has.

I run over to Jack, wagging my tail, and lick him.

'I'm so happy to see you. I was really worried,' I say.

'I expect you thought you wouldn't see me again, didn't you? Well, old Jack got better, thanks to Pip. He told the store manager about me and they took me off to the hospital, gave me a load of pills and now I'm as right as my left foot. And Pip just got a ticking off.'

In the morning, Pip leaves me with Jack.

'I'm going into town, Ray. I don't want anything to happen to you again, so you'd best stay here. Jack'll make sure you're all right.'

He hasn't left me before and I am anxious. Why can't I be with him? Has he stopped liking me?

I sit down next to Jack and watch Pip disappear across the car park.

'Don't worry, old girl,' says Jack, 'he'll be back. He's just gone to get something for you.'

Is it my birthday? What is the date today? Actually, when *was* my birthday?

I can't quite remember. I'm not trying to remember my birthday as a *dog* – because that would have been when we had the car crash and that was . . . Well, when was *that*? Was it Christmas time? Perhaps Dad and I were going to the supermarket to buy a turkey. I can't quite remember. No, it is my birthday as Daisy I am trying to remember. It sort of swims in and out of my memory like a goldfish.

I am still trying to remember my birthday when Pip comes back. He is carrying a small brown paper bag and is looking very pleased with himself.

'Here we are, Ray. You're official now. They won't take you away from me again.' And out of the bag he takes a bright blue collar and on the collar is a disc. And engraved on the disc in big letters is the word R A Y. This certainly *feels* like my birthday, whether it is or not.

'Thank you, Pip. I feel really special now,' I say.

But what is even better than *my* name is that on the back of the disc it says,

P I P.

Ray and Pip. I wear it like a locket round my neck. Ray and Pip. And it nestles on my fur close to my heart.

I want to know when we're going to look for Pip's dad. I think we've been in the station car park for too long. Besides, I can't remember the registration number of Dad's car any more and it bothers me. I'm sure he had a blue car but when I try to think of the number plate it all goes fuzzy. I think I need new horizons and some fresh air. Henry VIII's wives have completely escaped me now. This worries me. What will happen if I stop remembering who I really am?

It seems that Pip is trying to get some money to buy a train ticket. He has an idea that his father might be living in the same town where he and his mum went to college.

'We're going to find him, Ray! Even if I have to ring every number in the phone book!'

He's left me with Jack a few times to see if he can get any jobs. He's already swept an old lady's drive, cleaned a car and carried stuff to the dump. He's even been paid for walking some dogs! He found an old dog lead at the dump. He showed it to me.

'You'll have to wear this sometimes, Ray, when we go travelling.'

I looked at him. I hoped he could see my mouth turning down with disapproval.

Pip is coming towards me now along the station car park.

'I've got enough, Jack!' he says. 'We'll go tomorrow!'

And Jack nods his head and puts his hand on my back.

'It's time now, that's for sure. It'll be good for your soul to move on. I hope you find your dad. Don't forget to send old Jack a postcard!'

But we all know that Jack would never get it.

'I'll miss you, Jack,' I tell him. 'If it weren't for you I'd still be with Cyril and I'd never have tasted freedom. You've shown me what's possible in a dog's life.'

I nuzzle up to him. He smells of old books and newspapers and the sea. We sleep.

I dream Jack is in a large wooden sailing ship with acres of sails. He is at the helm and a huge wave hits the boat side on. Hundreds of silver fish are left flapping on the decks, and as the boat goes up and down the fish slide from side to side. I watch the ship sail away and as it goes over the horizon there is a green flash and Jack and the boat have gone.

We buy a ticket and get on the train. I'm not allowed on the seat but I jump up on it anyway so that I can look out of the window. I went in Cyril's car once to go to the vet and I was able to get my whole head out of the window. The feeling of the wind was wonderful. It felt like white-water rafting and abseiling and flying all at once. Not that I think I've done any of those things.

The guard goes past and I jump off the seat and hide under the table at Pip's feet.

'You got a ticket?' he asks.

I expect he thinks Pip can't afford a ticket.

'Yes,' Pip says, proudly showing it to the guard. I feel proud of Pip too.

The train stops several times before we get out.

'End of the line!' someone shouts, and we all tumble out onto the platform.

Chapter 7

This place is by the sea. I can smell the sea air and it puts a spring in my step.

'It's a bit late to make phone calls now, Ray,' Pip says to me. 'I don't have a mobile but we'll find a phone box and make a start in the morning. We'd better find somewhere to sleep.'

There is a pier and a long promenade by the beach. Down on the sand there is a fish and chip van. Pip has just enough money for a portion of chips and a saveloy sausage. He saves all his small change for the phone box. We sit on the beach and watch the waves breaking against the shore. Pip gives me half his sausage and some of his chips.

'Things'll get better, don't you worry,' he says.

But I *am* worried. I'm worried that Pip won't be able to find his dad and then he'll be taken back to his foster parents. I wouldn't be allowed to visit him *there*. I decide that if I can help it, I won't ever let Pip out of my sight. But before that I just have to have a paddle.

A bit of a breeze has blown up now. The beach is becoming deserted and we wander back into town. We walk down side streets and across squares until we come to the back of a huge hotel. There is a grate in the pavement with hot air blowing out of it.

'Here we are, Ray. We'll sleep here for the night.'

Pip takes out his sleeping bag and an old towel for me to sleep on. It's quite warm by the grate but there's a chill in the air. I give Pip's face a lick. It tastes salty. I can see a big tear rolling down his cheek.

'I miss Mum,' he whispers and makes room

111

for me in his sleeping bag. I crawl in next to him and rest my chin on his hand.

We are woken early by the seagulls screaming at the refuse lorry. We go back to the beach. I look in the bins that the refuse men haven't emptied yet. I'm surprised Pip doesn't want any of it. There's masses of good stuff in here. I hastily eat a potato skin and a stale currant bun. Really, I can't imagine why I was so disgusted by bins. They are a positive *haven* of things to eat. Even if it's just licking something off a bit of a paper bag.

When we reach the beach Pip throws stones into the sea. He makes them skim across the top of the water. I can still remember my dream about Jack and wonder if he's out there somewhere in a big wooden sailing ship with acres of sails. I see another dog on the sand and run off to chase it. Then the dog chases me and before we know it there are three or four other dogs all chasing each other. I hear Pip call, 'Ray! Come on!'

The other dogs know it's not a call for them and

carry on running round in circles. I'm proud that Pip is calling for me and I show off by sprinting very fast across the sand, shouting as I go.

'I'm here! Wait for me! Don't leave me!'

We are trying to find the library. There are so many things I have to have a good sniff at on the way. Simply masses of dogs I've never met and probably never will have left me messages on the lampposts and letterboxes. They don't usually say more than 'Hi! I was here and this is *my* lamppost.' Sometimes it's someone looking for a mate. I liken it to being on Facebook. This is *my* computer world now. It doesn't matter that it's not a worldwide web. It's small and intimate and how I like it. I have to leave the odd message as well, but I'm not letting Pip out of my sight so I can only leave one or two.

My vow to not let Pip out of my sight is short-lived. We find the local library and I have to let him go in on his own.

It's surprising how many people stop and talk to a dog on its own. I don't think anyone stops to talk to Pip. Except for the couple of men who

113

wanted to talk to him about Jesus.

So far ten people have patted me. Two people have asked me if I'm dangerous and will I bite them? And one person has given me the crusts of her sandwich.

At last Pip comes out of the library with a piece of paper on which he's written some numbers.

'There are four Seagroves!' he says excitedly, and we leave to find a phone box.

I jump up and down at his side. 'Well done, Pip! Well done!' I say as we race along the pavement. 'Perhaps they're *all* related to you!'

The first three boxes we find are all for cards or emergency numbers only.

'But this *is* an emergency,' I say. 'You should be able to ask the emergency services to find your dad.'

I'm not sure Pip is listening.

'Shhh, Ray. I'm trying to think,' he says.

Now we're at a phone box that takes coins and I can see Pip dialling the first number. There is no one there, just an answer machine. Pip puts down the phone and tries another number. I can hear the number ringing. It is in time with my heartbeat, which seems to have quickened with anticipation. A voice is at the other end.

'Hello,' says Pip. 'Does a Phillip Seagrove live there?'

I thought *he* was Phillip Seagrove. I feel a bit confused. Perhaps he has the same name as his dad. I can hear the voice at the other end say, 'No. No one of that name here.' And then the sound of the dialling tone again.

The third number has a *number not recognised* message on it. Pip gets an answer on the fourth.

'*Phillip* Seagrove?' the voice says. 'No, I'm *Daphne* Seagrove.'

'Are you any relation?' asks Pip. 'Do you *know* a Phillip Seagrove?'

'Now let me think,' the voice continues. 'I think my mother may have had a cousin called Phillip. But he wouldn't have been a Seagrove, of course. Anyway he'd be dead by now. I'm nearly ninety! You wouldn't think it, would you? Perhaps it was Patrick, not Phillip. Sorry, dear, I can't help you.' And the line went dead. Pip sighed.

'OK, Ray. Two out of four, an answerphone and a number not recognised. We'll have to try again, but I've run out of cash.'

He seems disheartened. We are back at the grate behind the hotel again. There are a couple of men already there with bottles of cider. They seem harmless enough, but Pip won't let me check them out. We've found some out-of-date sandwiches behind a takeaway bar.

'It's my birthday tomorrow, Ray,' Pip says as he hands me a ham sandwich. 'This is my first birthday without Mum. She always made me a birthday cake. Chocolate, usually, cos that's my favourite. She gave me this watch last year.'

He takes a watch out of his bag.

'It's lovely,' I tell him. 'It even has a date on, doesn't it?'

I'm trying to think of *my* last birthday but I can't even remember if I *had* a cake. When I think of it it's like there is an empty space in my memory where my birthday used to be. And if I think too hard about it there's a sort of buzzing sensation in my mind, like an angry insect is guarding the empty space from the memory.

In the morning I cover him with kisses.

'Happy birthday, Pip,' I say to him. If I was a cat I would go off and catch him a little mouse as a present. But what can I give him?

We go to the beach. There's no one on it and the tide is beginning to come in. There is a line of plastic bottles and seaweed and bits of driftwood and bits of fishing nets and empty crab shells. All good to sniff at. Pip puts down his bag and begins to take off his jacket.

'I've just got to go and have a swim. It's tradition, you see. I always have this urge to go into water on my birthday. My mum used to say I was trying to get back into the womb.'

'But it's too cold to swim now. What if you get cramp?' I say to him.

There is a plimsoll washed up with the seaweed and I go and fetch it. I start running around him with it in my mouth and drop it in front of him. I don't want him going in the sea. I think it's too dangerous. When I see he's not going to throw the shoe, I go and fetch a piece of the driftwood.

'Come on, Ray, just sit here by my clothes and guard the bag.'

I look around me. In the distance I can see a figure walking but it is a long way away. Otherwise it doesn't seem as if there is anyone on the beach. Pip takes off all his clothes except his underpants and then runs into the surf.

'Come back!' I shout.

He dives into the waves and disappears from sight. I get up, anxious that he won't surface again, but there he is a little further out, grinning and waving at me. He starts swimming. He is a strong swimmer and soon he is quite far out.

'Come back!' I shout again. I leave the bag and run along the shoreline. How can I keep an eye on him if he swims so far out? My paws are wet now. It's not as cold as I thought it would be, so I run a bit further in. But Pip is swimming further and further away.

I strike out after him and shout at him to stop and be careful and watch what he's doing. The current is quite strong and although I am swimming straight at him I can feel I am being swept further down along the beach. How am I going to rescue him and bring him back to safety if he keeps swimming away?

Pip's bag looks a long way away now. And so does Pip. A big wave sweeps over my head and sucks me down. I'm caught up in it and my body is turning over and over and I'm not sure which way is up. I'm holding my breath but I can feel it leaving my body and my lungs ache now. I've got my eyes open to see which way is up but the water is cloudy with lots of grit and sand flying past.

At last I bob up to the surface. My paws are paddling hard to keep me above the water. I look around me. Pip's bag is now a speck on the beach and it looks as if he is standing by it because I can see a figure bending down.

Good. I can relax a little. I can stop worrying about both Pip and his bag. But then I hear a shout and there is Pip *swimming towards me*.

Another wave gets hold of me and hurls me onto the shingle.

'Ray! You silly dog. You didn't have to come in after me. I was coming back.'

'But Pip!' I choke, spitting the seaweed out of my mouth. 'Who's with the bag?'

Although I know Pip doesn't understand me, something causes him to look along the beach and we both see someone making off with Pip's bag.

'Oh no!' He curses and starts to run up the beach. 'Everything I own is in that bag. It's all I have.'

I struggle to my feet and run after him, but the weight of the water in my fur slows me down. I have to stop and shake it off and I lose valuable seconds. This really is all my fault. If only I had stayed with the bag and not been so keen to keep up with Pip. He was right. I am indeed a silly dog.

It's a man who has the bag and he's walking fast along the beach with it tucked under his arm.

'Stop! That's my bag!' yells Pip.

The man turns for a moment and then quickens his pace. There is still quite a gap between us. I am now running flat out. I'm faster than Pip and determined to get the bag, even though I remember it's got my lead in it. It has Pip's watch in it as well and I want him to always know when his birthday is. I can't remember mine any more.

The man with the bag is running now but he is not sure on his feet and stumbles on the stones.

'Come back with that bag!' I yell. 'It doesn't belong to you and it's got Pip's whole world in it.'

But the man gets up and keeps running. He is wearing loose trousers and the hem is flapping as he runs. All my muscles are working in my body now and I feel as if I am eating up the distance between us. I am close enough now and I get ready to leap. I spring from my back legs and I soar through the air. The force of my jump pulls my mouth back and with a snap of my teeth I get hold of the trousers. My jaws may not be good for bubblegum but they certainly work when you want to get hold of a trouser leg.

There is a ripping sound and the man falls onto the shingle. I see a bare ankle and I fasten my teeth on it. He smells stale, of alcohol and fear.

The man yells out, 'Get that crazy dog off me!' And Pip races up to my side. He grabs the bag off the man before he says to me, 'That's enough, Ray. Leave him.'

Reluctantly I let go of the man's ankle. He scrambles up. He has a wild look in his eyes and a tattoo of a snake winding round his neck. I back off. There's something about the snake I don't like and although I know it's not real I'm going to keep my distance now in case it suddenly comes alive.

'I fought it 'ad bin left. I fought it didn't belong to no one.' He has a thin, whiney voice and he backs away from us, looking for somewhere to run.

'Well it does!' yells Pip. 'It belongs to me. Go away and leave us alone or I'll set my dog on you again!'

At this I show him my teeth and I shout at him, 'Yes! Clear off and leave us alone!'

He's running now, back up the beach, not fast, because he's limping a bit. I look at Pip and wag my tail.

'Clever Ray!' says Pip. I like it when he praises me and I put my ears flat back so that he can stroke my head properly. I feel much braver about the snake now.

We go back to where Pip's clothes are and he takes the picture of his dad out of his pocket and looks at it. I realise that this is the most important thing that he has. Apart from me, that is.

We follow in the footsteps of the man and I have a good sniff at his prints. I still have the image of his snake and half expect to find its track on the sand as well. All that seawater I swallowed must be playing tricks with my mind. It's not a big town and I hope we don't see him again. Even with my new-found braveness, I'm not sure I could fight off more than one person if he happened to have some friends. This is going to give me something else to worry about.

There's something fluttering along the sand in front of us. I run to catch it. It's a folded-up piece of paper. I pick it up to show Pip. Neither Pip nor I can stand people throwing litter on the ground. It brings out the policewoman in me.

'What's this, Ray?' he says, taking the paper out of my mouth.

'Crikey!' he says. 'It's a twenty-pound note!'

He dances around me and I join in.

'Twenty pounds! What a fantastic birthday present, Ray! Well done!'

My tail is now going round and round like a propeller and I think I might take off. This is better than presenting him with a little mouse.

'I think that man dropped it when he was running away. I expect he stole it from someone else. Like he took our bag,' I tell him.

Pip looks around.

'There's no one to give it back to. So I think we'll *have* to keep it. HAPPY BIRTHDAY, PIP!' he shouts.

'HAPPY BIRTHDAY, PIP!' I shout back.

We run along the beach and back into town.

'We'll have to buy something so that I can get more change for the telephone,' he says. Then I can see his eyes light up. 'And I know just what it's going to be!'

I follow him up the side streets. There's a lovely smell coming from a shop a few doors along.

'Stay here, Ray,' Pip says as he goes inside.

I look into the shop. It is full of loaves of bread and pastries and smells absolutely delicious. In a few minutes Pip comes out carrying a white box tied up with ribbon.

'Come on! Back to the beach!' he yells to me, and we retrace our footsteps and go and sit under the pier and Pip opens the box and inside is a large, beautiful chocolate cake.

Chapter 8

When Pip gets through to the answerphone number a man with a thick foreign accent answers.

'Hello,' says Pip, speaking slowly and rather loudly in case the man doesn't understand him. 'Does a Phillip Seagrove live there?'

There is a pause on the other end of the line.

'No. Very sorry. Mr Seagrove passed away a year now.'

Pip catches his breath and says, 'Oh no! That can't be. How can he die when I haven't found him yet?'

I'm not sure if he's talking to himself or the

man on the phone but the voice on the other end continues.

'Well,' the voice says, 'he was very old and been ill some time.'

'How old?' asks Pip.

'I am thinking eighty-something.'

Pip sighs with relief.

'Oh, not *my* Mr Seagrove then. Did he have a son, do you think?'

'Oh no, no. Mr Seagrove, he having no family. I had to make all arrangement for him.'

'I am sorry,' says Pip. 'But thank you.'

He looks pleased until he realises he is still no closer to finding his father. He tries the *number not recognised* again and gets the same recorded message.

'You know what, Ray? We're going to go round to the address in the phone book, just in case the number has been changed.'

The address is in Barton Road.

'Let's find a map,' says Pip, excited again.

I'm excited too. I want Pip to find his dad. I'm trying to picture *my* dad now.

He has a hat and coat and no face and a car with a registration number that I cannot possibly remember.

Barton Road is up a long hill and full of white-washed houses. When we get to the top we look back over the bay. There are a few fishing boats and someone water-skiing. It's practically midwinter and I tell Pip that I think the water-skier must be mad. He'd be sure to get hyperthermia if he fell in.

Number twelve has a little front gate and a well-tended front garden. Pip waits outside for a while.

'Go on, Pip,' I say. 'Go and knock on the door.'

'I'm feeling nervous, Ray. What if he answers the door? I'd have liked to speak to him on the phone first. What if he doesn't accept I'm his son?'

Then Pip pauses a moment and adds, 'What if we don't like each other?'

I tell him I'm sure they will and search my brain for any clues that I had liked *my* father. But my memory seems a bit blocked and I can't even remember what he did for a living.

We've been hanging around the gate for some time now. I notice a woman with white hair by the net curtains, looking at us.

'Go *on*, Pip,' I say.

'Be quiet, Ray. You'll disturb the neighbours.'

But too late now. The door opens and the woman appears.

'Can I help you, dear?' she says. 'Are you looking for someone?'

'Yes,' says Pip. 'Does Phillip Seagrove live here?'

'Ah, no,' the woman replies and I know Pip's heart has sunk, just like mine. 'But I still have a forwarding address, I think, if you just hang on a moment.'

She goes back into the house and is gone for some time. Pip shifts his weight from foot to foot. Takes his hands out of his pockets, then puts them in again. Then takes them out. He opens and shuts the gate several times.

'Sorry about that,' says the woman when she returns with a piece of paper. 'It was at the back of one of the drawers. They moved out about a year ago now.' She hands Pip the paper.

'*They?*' he says.

'Yes. A really nice family. They have a little boy.'

I notice Pip stiffen.

'Any dogs?' I ask.

The woman strokes me. 'Are you being ignored? I had a dog like you once, with those coloured eyes. A collie called Jessie.'

'Was she a spirit dog?' I ask. But the lady is on her way back inside.

'Where is this?' Pip calls out.

'It's just along the coast, dear. Not too far! Good luck!'

Pip turns the paper over in his hands.

'Well, Ray. Looks as if we might find him after all.' But I can tell he's not as pleased as I thought he'd be.

We walk off down the road and I wonder if Pip knows where we are going.

Pip's still got change from the twenty-pound note and suggests we go into a café and have something to eat. We pass one now. There is a tantalising smell of bacon cooking on a big stove and a moussaka that has just been taken out of the oven.

'Moussaka!' I say. 'My favourite, after . . . well.' That busy insect is back again, daring me to remember my other favourite dishes. I give up and sniff at a lamppost.

'Come on, Ray, let's have something to eat.'

'You can't bring that dog in here,' says the man cutting up the moussaka.

'OK,' Pip says, sounding disappointed. 'We'll go then.'

I want to say to him that it doesn't matter. I'm quite happy to sit outside the café. I want him to have something to eat because I worry he's not getting enough vitamins. I'm beginning to sound like my mum. But Mum's face doesn't come to mind as it used to and all I get is a glimpse of an apron with 'I'm the Boss' written on it.

I suddenly feel weary and don't see the point in telling Pip all this if he can't understand what I'm saying.

'We do takeaway!' the man says as we start to leave the café.

We are sitting on some rocks under the pier,

sharing a portion of moussaka.

'You know, Ray,' Pip tells me, in between mouthfuls. 'I've been thinking of Dad for all this time, since Mum died, and I don't know what I imagined but I hadn't thought of him with another family. I thought he'd be on his own, like me, and that he'd be pleased to have the company. Now I'm a bit afraid he won't want us cos he'll be too busy with his other family. And what if his wife doesn't like me? She'll probably be cross with him for getting another woman pregnant before her.'

I rest my head in his lap and look up at him.

'It'll be fine, Pip. He won't turn you away.' I want to add that he may turn *me* away. What if they have a dog like that jealous Moss? Two dogs is one dog too many. But I keep that to myself.

We spend our night behind the hotel. There is quite a gathering of people there now and it's noisy. Pip and I curl up together. I dream of the man with the tattoo. I dream that the snake uncoils itself from around the man's neck and slithers after me. I try to run, but in my dream

I've eaten too much chocolate cake and cannot move. The snake flicks out its tongue and bites me in the stomach.

I wake up with a yelp and a feeling that my belly is on fire. Pip is not in good shape either and he has his knees up on his chest and is moaning softly. He looks rather ashen. He sees me looking at him.

'I feel *awful*, Ray. I want to be sick but I can't with all these people around. I think I need some fresh air. Let's move down to the pier.'

There is no one around as we make our way slowly to the beach. Pip is bent double most of the way and continues to moan to himself. He's sick several times behind a rock. I'm sick in some seaweed and feel much better for it. I decide that moussaka is no longer my favourite food.

Pip splashes seawater on his face and then drags his things up the beach, gets his sleeping bag out and gets in it. There is an overwhelming smell of rotting fish and seaweed but he doesn't seem to care. I lick his face to make him feel better but he's got his eyes shut now. I think of Jack when he was ill. How can *I* get pills for Pip?

I stay with him and watch the sunrise. A few early-morning walkers arrive on the beach, but we are hidden from view and when I get up and look back at Pip in his sleeping bag he just looks like another rock.

I decide to get help. There is a jogger coming along the beach. I run towards him.

'Can you help us?' I say. 'My Pip is ill and I think he needs a doctor or to go to hospital or something.'

The jogger has earphones in and is listening to music. I don't think he can hear me. I jump up at him as he's running along but he just kicks out at me and waves his arms.

'Shooooo!' he says and puts on a spurt of speed. I want to nip his stupid Lycra-clad legs. I won't help *him* if he's ever in trouble. I watch him run and think how ridiculous humans look sometimes.

I try a couple of other people but they think I want to play with them and throw things into the sea for me. I'm too polite to ignore them so I go and fetch the things back but I can't get them to follow me. What shall I do? I shout my frustration at the waves and begin to make my way back to Pip. He looks very pale and seems to be asleep. I hope he's not dead. I put my nose near his mouth and feel my whiskers tickled by his breath. At least he's alive. But what am I going to do?

I remember the nice old lady who gave us Pip's dad's address. She's the only person we've had proper contact with in this town. Surely if I could find her house again, she would come and help Pip?

But I am torn. How can I leave him? What if something happens to him while I am away? What if he wakes up and finds I've gone? He might be feeling better and get up and go, and then I might never see him again. I sit down next to him and wait.

After a while I think I'll try to wake him.

'Pip,' I say, nudging him gently. 'I think I'd better go and get some help.'

Pip opens his eyes and stares at me. I don't think he knows who I am.

'Pip! It's me. Ray. I'm going to go and fetch that

lady who lives in your dad's old house.'

'Why are you whining at me?' Pip slurs. 'I can't come and play with you cos I feel too ill. Can't you find another dog to play with?' And he pulls his sleeping bag up over his ears and goes back to sleep.

Well, that's that then. I'm going to have to find that old lady. I'll just have to hope that he doesn't move before I come back.

I retrace our steps. Back to the grate outside the hotel. Back to the spot on the beach where we ate. I can hardly bring myself to think of what we ate in case I'm sick again. I know this is a backwards way of doing it but I can't remember the route to the restaurant unless I do *exactly* what we did the night before. Anyway, we didn't sit on this exact same spot of the beach, so I don't feel quite so silly.

From the beach I take another route. I can smell the café from round the corner. Breakfast. Green bacon and soggy toast. I feel like telling them they ought to be closed down for food poisoning, but I'm in a hurry.

Then where did we come from? I remember we ambled a bit and I hadn't thought that Pip knew where we were going. Why do all these roads look the same? Barton Road! Where are you?

I steer clear of the newspaper boy. I'd like to ask him the way but I know what will happen, so I keep going. And I'm not stopping to sniff anything either, even though quite a few dogs have already been out, even this early in the morning.

Thank goodness I can still read. After a false alarm with a Barnaby Road, I see the sign.

I race up the pavement and reach the gate. What now? Old ladies probably sleep in late. She's probably deaf too and may not sleep with her hearing aid in. Nevertheless. Time is not on my side. I jump up and over the wall.

'Wake up! Wake up! I need help here. Come to the door and you'll see who it is!'

I jump up against the door, willing it to fall open.

'Stop that wretched barking!' A man in pyjamas pulls down the window of the next-door house. 'Some of us are trying to sleep!'

But I carry on. I have to get her attention.

And I do.

I was expecting her to be wearing her nightie but she is fully dressed.

'Hello! It's *you*! Where's your friend? That nice boy you were with?'

'He's ill. Terribly ill. Could you help me, please? If you follow me I'll show you where he is, cos I don't really know what to do. We ate some dodgy moussaka from a café last night and although I've not been feeling too good, Pip is much worse than me.'

'Can't you shut that dog up?' The man in pyjamas is back at his window again.

'Sorry, Mr Pettigrew.' The old lady looks up. 'I'll take him inside with me.'

'I'm a girl, actually, not a boy,' I say. 'I can't come in the house. You've got to follow me. Please come! He's very ill. He needs help.' I run round in circles, trot a little way to the gate and go back to her side. I repeat this several times.

'Oh dear, oh dear. What's the matter? Has something happened?' She looks up at Mr

Pettigrew's window. 'Won't be a minute!' she calls up to him. 'I think the dog's a bit distressed.'

She turns back to me.

'Oh dear. I don't know what to do. I think you're trying to tell me something, aren't you?'

I wag my tail at her, encouragingly.

'Is it that you want me to follow you?'

'Yes!' I bark.

The wonderful woman fetches her coat and follows me down the road. I go back to her every now and then to make sure she is still coming. We go onto the beach and I race over to the rocks. Pip is just where I left him with his eyes still shut.

'Oh, you poor boy,' she says when she sees him. 'What's happened?'

I lick Pip's face and he opens his eyes. They look red and watery. I don't think he realises it's the woman we've been to see but he manages to speak and tells her he's eaten something bad.

'Well, my boy,' she says. 'You'd better come back with me and I'll see what I can do. Can you walk a little way? No, perhaps not. If you stay here with your dog I'll go back and fetch my car.

If you can manage to get to it I can drive you back home and you can lie on a proper bed. I've got some very good medicine for sickness. Will you be all right for a short while? I'm Marjorie, by the way.'

Chapter 9

Marjorie's house is warm and comfortable and simply packed with pictures of her dog, Jessie. I look into the dog's eyes in a framed photo and I see my eyes staring back.

'You can sleep on her old blanket if you like,' she says to me. 'For some reason I've kept it, and her travel rug is still in my car. Silly of me really, isn't it? I'll put it down in front of the fire and, Pip, you can have the bed in the spare room.' And she makes him comfortable and gives him her very good medicine and pours me a bowl of milk.

'It's been a long time since I've had a dog lie

in front of that fire. I miss Jessie, you know, Ray. She understood everything I said to her. Like I get the feeling *you* do. Is that right?'

I wag my tail.

'Did she frighten farm animals?' I ask her. But she just smiles at me and looks after Pip.

'You and Ray best stay here for a while, Pip, to get your strength up before starting your journey. I am planning on driving you there myself, if you like. To save you the travelling. I don't go out in the car much and a little journey in the countryside will do me and the car some good.'

Relief seems to flood over Pip's face. I wag my tail at him. Marjorie's going to make him better, I know.

Pip sleeps for two days. He tosses and turns and I watch his colour change from very pale to warm pink again. I don't tell Marjorie in case she thinks I'm ungrateful, but when she goes to bed I lie outside Pip's door in case he needs me.

Marjorie takes me for early-morning walks before breakfast while he is still recovering and I trot along happily at her side, knowing Pip is getting well. She is very tolerant and doesn't seem to mind me stopping every so often to find who's been about.

'I can't see the point in sleeping my life away, Ray,' she tells me as we walk along the road. 'I probably don't have long now. I'm really quite old.' She bends down and gives me a pat. 'I'm not afraid of dying, you know.'

I want to tell her about the Job Centre and the woman behind the desk and to make sure she goes through the wrong door if she wants to remember who she is, but I can't put it into words for her. So I just wag my tail.

'When my husband passed away I got Jessie as a puppy from a farmer. He didn't want her on his farm. So she came to *me*.'

I like this story. It means there are probably lots of dogs like me out there, with strange eyes. And the farmer probably didn't want her because his cows were freaked out by her eyes. I want to believe Jack's story of spirit dogs.

'My husband was never very keen on dogs and would never let me have one when he was alive. Actually, he was a very grumpy person. He hardly ever spoke to me. And I had no one to talk to. When Jessie came along it was quite a different story. It was just like having another person living with me, but one who enjoyed my company, never criticised me and was always pleased to see me!'

I think of Jack and how lovely it would be if he and Marjorie could be together. I think they would have a lot to talk about. But how could I tell her about this old man a train journey away, who may not even be alive?

We stay with Marjorie for a week. Pip plays cards with her in the evenings and we all settle down together on her sofa to watch the television. It's been ages since I've seen a television. I particularly like the wildlife programmes. I think neither of us has ever eaten so well either. She makes lovely hotpots for Pip and gives me the gravy, with some biscuits for tea.

Then one day Pip decides it's time we went on our way. He has the address of his father burning a hole in his pocket, I think, and can wait no longer. He finally tells Marjorie his story. She puts her arms around him.

'I'm determined to drive you there, dear. I don't want you having to tramp the streets again.' Marjorie goes out to check the oil and petrol in her car and minutes later comes in, looking flustered.

'My car has gone! Where my car was is an empty space! I can't think what's happened to it.'

'Do you think you parked it somewhere else and have forgotten where?' asks Pip.

'Well dear, I don't think so. When I parked it I remember thinking the passenger door was a bit near the lamppost. The lamppost is still there – but not my car! There's been a spate of car thefts recently. I'd better tell the police.'

Pip is worried about the police seeing him and taking him back to the foster parents and says he had better hide somewhere if they come round.

'Well dear, if you're really worried I'll ring the police after you've gone. So, as I can't drive you, I'm going to give you my old bicycle. I expect the tyres need pumping up. I don't use it any more.

It's mainly country lanes to get to your father's so you should be all right. Is that a good idea?'

Pip nods and I'm thrilled. It means lots of things to sniff at on the way and a chance to really stretch my legs. Pip pumps up the tyres and Marjorie gives him a pack of sandwiches.

'There's a little something for you as well, Ray.'

'Thank you, thank you!' I say to her. 'You've been so kind and saved my Pip. I hope you get another dog one day.'

'Ah, my dears!' she says. 'It's been lovely knowing you. Don't forget to come and visit if you're this way again.' And she strokes my head and hugs Pip, and we set off down the road.

There is a wintry sun out and I'm excited. Pip flashes me a grin as he freewheels down the hill. We are soon out of the town and in open countryside. I keep on the inside of Pip when we are on a busy stretch of road, but as soon as we get to the quiet lanes I'm all over the place. There is so much to smell. Simply loads of animals have been along the lanes. A badger has been here, a fox has left his scent there, and I nearly catch a pheasant that is pecking by the roadside. Really, they are such stupid birds. I'm glad I didn't come back as a *pheasant*. If they didn't draw attention to themselves by flapping their wings and screeching you wouldn't notice them half the time. This one is so fat it can hardly get up into the air and I manage to grab one of its tail feathers before it finally takes off. I give the feather to Pip and he puts it in his hat.

Sometimes I get left behind a bit if there is a particularly good smell, but Pip calls my name and it's my chance to tear along the road and make my ears fly again. We stop for sandwiches. Marjorie has put in those little bone-shaped biscuits for me. How happy I am to see them! It's funny what you take for granted. I wasn't too pleased with them at Cyril's, but I haven't seen them in so long I eat them excitedly. The last one I had was outside my old house in Alexander Avenue. I realise I can remember everything as a dog with great clarity, but when I try to picture my bedroom again I have absolutely no idea what it looked like. I just have some vague memory of a swirling pink net.

We continue along the road. Suddenly a hare dashes out in front of Pip's bicycle. He wobbles and I think falls off the bike but I'm after the hare before I've had time to think. How *dare* it cause my Pip to come off the bike? What does it think it's doing? And it hasn't even stopped to see if Pip is all right. And although I haven't stopped to see if Pip is all right either I'm off to have words with it.

It's gone through the hedge and out the other side and I have too. It's the fastest thing I've ever chased and every time I think I'm nearly on it it zigzags across the field and I've lost valuable seconds. I think I can hear Pip's voice calling me but my concentration is on catching the hare and I can't possibly stop now. I think I really am flying again. My paws hardly touch the ground. There is still stubble in this field that pricks my paws when I do touch down, but the next has been ploughed. The one after is rough grass and then I lose the hare! Where has it gone? There is a big crater in the middle of the field filled with brambles and old, rusty pieces of farm machinery and the hare has gone to ground somewhere in it, I'm now sure. I spend ages sniffing around for it and then finally give up.

I suddenly remember Pip. Where is he? I scan the horizon and all I can see is fields. No road. No bike. I've probably been gone ages. I don't seem to have any sense of time any more. I try to run back the way I came, but I'm panting so much now I've stopped that I can only manage a limping trot. My tongue is hanging out as far as I can get it and I'm trying to catch my breath too. I cross the ploughed field but I'm not sure which stubble field I've crossed. There seems to be rather a lot of them. And now a wind has blown up and if Pip *were* calling me I wouldn't stand a chance of hearing him.

I begin to panic. How can I have been so stupid as to chase that hare? How can I have left Pip after my vow never to let him out of my sight? And the more I think about the hare I realise that the instincts of being a dog are taking over the instincts of being Daisy. And it scares me.

I haven't a clue where I am now. I see a road

winding its way between some fields in the distance and make my way towards it. With any luck it'll be Pip's road. To get to it I have to go through a hedge and over a ditch and as I emerge I see something big and metal poking out of the hedge on the other side. I cross the road to check it out. It's a car with its back wheels in the ditch and its front wheels through the hedge. I wonder if there is someone still in the car but the door is open and I can't smell anyone around. I look inside. On the back seat is a rug. A red-and-black checked rug. I remember Marjorie telling me that she still kept Jessie's travelling rug in her car. This is definitely Marjorie's missing car!

I really want to tell Marjorie where her car is but I'm not exactly sure I know. I am hoping this is the road Pip is on, but has he passed the car or not reached it yet? He probably won't know what Marjorie's car looks like, he was so ill when he travelled in it. And now it's beginning to rain! Big fat drops are falling on me now. *Pitter. Patter.* I hate getting wet. So I jump into Marjorie's car and try to settle down.

Someone's been in the car who doesn't smell good.

I feel my hackles begin to rise. The smell reminds me of being on the beach. Yes! That's it. *The snake man.* This car definitely smells of him!

I get up at once and carefully look under the seats in case he's still in the car and hiding.

He's not there.

I put my nose into the tartan rug. Yes, there's Marjorie's dog smell – I remember it from the rug in the house. Very faint, because it must have been ages since she lay on this travel rug. She smells like a kind dog. Caramel and wool. She smells like she was a good age. I settle down on the red-and-black tartan rug and wait for Pip.

Oh dear, poor Pip – he is going to be soaked through by now. If only he could get here quickly and take shelter in the car. I hear thunder in the distance and I shiver. I've never liked thunderstorms and now I'm a dog I seem to hate them even more. I can't stop my body from shaking and I'm whimpering and fretting now, which I find a bit pathetic, but I can't control it.

What if Pip meets the snake man on the road? The wind has begun to shriek through the trees.

The rain is absolutely pouring down and banging on the roof. It's like being inside a tin drum. *Clatter, clatter, thud, thud.* I don't want Pip to catch a chill. I strain my ears for the whirr of a bicycle wheel but nothing passes. I can hear the gasp of a mouse in the hedgerow, though, and the high-pitched whine of some flying insect. This hearing lark is fantastic.

Eventually the storm blows over and a watery afternoon sun pokes out from behind the clouds. There is a hushed stillness. I get out of Marjorie's car and decide to continue along the road to look for Pip. It's a quiet road and only one or two cars have passed me going the other way. A blue transit van overtakes me, splashing me with a puddle. *Swish. Swoosh. Squelch. Squeal.* It slams on its brakes a little way in front of me. A woman gets out.

Now, the Daisy part of me issues a warning. Don't talk to strangers and never get into a car with someone you don't know. But the dog part of me is pleased to see someone and my tail just wags all on its own.

'Hello, little dog,' the woman says, holding out her hand. 'Ain't yer got no 'ome? You're a fine dog, ain't yer? Who do yer belong to then?'

A man gets out of the van and shouts to her. 'Don't it belong to no one then?'

She strokes my head and reads the disc around my neck.

'Ray and Pip. Don't seem to 'ave no number or address. Don't know if the dog is Ray *or* Pip. But it looks like a stray to me. We might as well take it. Come on – I've got a nice treat for you in the van.'

I obediently follow her. I can see no point in telling her I'm not a stray and, after all, we might pass Pip on the way. Besides, I'm feeling a bit peckish now I've stopped all that panting.

I jump into the van and the woman gives me a ginger biscuit. The van smells of cigarettes and far away places. I give it a full examination and then settle down in the front so that I can look out of the window.

We drive along the road at various speeds. When the man is lighting a cigarette he slows right down and when he's finished he speeds up. I feel like telling him he shouldn't smoke. That by smoking he's shortening his life and ours by being in the van with him. But I don't feel like chatting. I'm keeping an eye out for Pip.

After a while they begin to argue about Marjorie's car and whether or not they should tell the police they've seen a car in the ditch. Then the man turns up the radio and some loud music blares out. I don't like it and busy myself looking out of the window. I want them to wind it down so that I can get my head out again but the man's put the heater on and I suppose they don't want to sit in a draught.

We drive along, the man tapping his hands on the steering wheel in time to the music and the woman singing to herself. As we go round a bend in the road I see a bicycle ahead.

'Stop! Stop the van! It's Pip! There he is! On the bicycle. Let me out. I belong to Pip. I must get to him.' I am scratching at the door now, trying to get out.

'What's that dog barking for?' says the man. 'Shut that barking up, will you?'

But I'm not going to give up that easily. I am desperate now. The van passes Pip on the bicycle. 'Stop! Stop! Let me OUT!'

I race from one side of the van to the other, making as much noise as possible. The man driving the car is beginning to look cross.

Pip is cycling furiously along the road. I'm not sure if he's seen me. If only I could have got my head out of the window. I'm in this blue van and he doesn't know. I feel part of me is lost without him and I'm pretty sure he is feeling the same thing. He's probably calling my name, hoping I can hear. But I can't, because the radio is on and I can't do anything about it. I start to wail. Long, painful sobs that echo round the inside of the empty van.

'We shouldn't have picked that dog up,' says the man, taking his eyes off the road to look at me.

'Aw – why not? 'E's a nice doggie. 'E'll shut up sooner or later – won't you, PipRay?'

But I continue to whine and we carry on driving,

getting further and further away from my Pip.

Then I hear a new noise. *Fizz. Sizzle. Splutter. Seethe. Sigh.* The van starts to bump and veer into the centre of the road.

'Blast!' says the driver. 'We've got a flat! Why do you always get a bleedin' puncture when it rains?'

He pulls to the side of the road and turns off the engine.

'I've got a jack in the back,' he says, and I hear him coming round to the rear door. I'm ready. I know there will only be a second before his frame fills the gap left when he opens the door. *Click.* The handle turns and I fly out. Launching myself into the rainy, grey space. I hit the road at a run. I'm not hanging around to be caught again. I can hear the woman cry out and the van driver say, 'Aw, let him go. He makes too much racket.'

And I race back the way we've come.

'Pip! Pip!' I'm shouting. 'It's me! RAY!' I am tearing along, ignoring the rabbits that scuttle back into the hedgerow and the crow, pecking at something dead in the road. And there in the distance is a little figure cycling through the puddles and it's my dear Pip. And when he sees me he drops his bike and I run towards him and he runs towards me and we're in each other's arms.

'I thought I'd never see you again, Ray.' He covers me in kisses and wipes his nose. I look at him and I see he's been crying.

Chapter 10

We are on top of a hill now and looking down on the town where Pip's dad lives. People are turning their lights on and shafts of smoke are rising from the chimneys. I can see quite well at night, better than when I was Daisy. I can make out each building. I can see people in the road. I can see dogs out on walks. I can see a television set flickering in an upstairs room.

'It's too late to try now,' decides Pip. 'We must find somewhere to sleep. I think we'd better stay out here and cycle down into town in the morning. Come on. There are some bushes over there we can crawl under.'

'I'll keep you warm, Pip,' I tell him, and we make our camp under the bush and I turn round and round for him to make sure there are no snakes hiding and to make it really comfy for him. We eat the remains of Marjorie's sandwiches and the last little bone biscuit.

We have a restless night. I think Pip has a nightmare because he's talking in his sleep and making groaning noises. I lick his nose to reassure him that everything is all right.

When we get down to the town in the morning, we see some toilets by the beach and Pip goes in and washes and brushes his hair and teeth. Marjorie has washed his clothes and in spite of a night sleeping rough I think Pip looks really presentable and I feel proud of him. Further up into town we see a newspaper boy outside a newsagent's shop and Pip asks him where Fielding Road is. I smile at the boy, in case he thinks I'm going to tug on his trouser cuff.

We are climbing up a hill again. Fielding Road is a bit like Marjorie's road and I wonder why Pip's dad has bothered to move. Perhaps it's something to do with his work, I think.

'Look, Ray!' says Pip excitedly. 'That must be it! The one with the mauve paintwork and the blue door. It looks the nicest house on the whole street, doesn't it?'

'Yes,' I say positively. 'It's a pretty colour, isn't it?'

I wonder what Pip is going to do. I'm all for marching straight up and getting it over with. But Pip seems to think otherwise.

'I'm going to wait a bit. See what he looks like.'

You know what he looks like. He looks like his picture, I think. But I don't say anything.

We hide the bike behind some bushes further up the road and stand on the other side of the street behind a parked car. We wait. We wait a long time. I've seen signs of life, curtains and windows opening. I think I see a child's face at a window, but I'm not sure. Then the door opens and a man steps out.

'That's him!' whispers Pip.

I don't think it looks like him at all. His hair

isn't that nice dark colour it was in the photo and he doesn't seem to have so much of it. Still, he looks nice and that's all that counts.

'Well, go on then! Aren't you going to say something?'

'Come on, Ray. Let's follow him. I'm not ready to speak to him yet. After all, he's not expecting us.'

The man doesn't seem to have a dog, much to my relief, and he sets off down the hill. He doesn't dawdle and I imagine he has a busy office to get to.

Pip and I follow behind him.

Eventually he turns into a small street that leads into a busier part of town. The streets are narrower and packed with interesting-looking shops. Lots of places selling books, musical instruments and Indian crafts. The man stops outside a brightly painted shop. Pip looks with interest in the window of the bookshop next door.

The man talks to a girl inside the shop as he opens the door.

'Thanks for opening up, Maisie. Sam was poorly and I wanted to let Viv sleep in a bit. She was up with him most of the night.'

Through the glass a pretty girl with a pile of pink hair smiles at him.

'That's OK. Is he better now?'

The man shuts the door behind him.

After a while, a delicious smell begins to waft out from the shop, and as the street begins to fill up, several people open the door and go in. We creep near to have a look. It is the most beautifully decorated door, with black-and-white stripes, and above it are the words: CAFÉ ZOO.

We stand outside for a good twenty minutes, stepping aside every time someone enters.

'What shall we do?' says Pip. 'I feel too nervous to go in and I've only got fifty pence.' But before I can answer him the girl with the pink hair comes to the door.

'Phil says do you want to come in? You can bring your dog if you like.'

'Yes please!' I bark and wag my tail at her. I'm going to give a good impression so that Pip's father likes me and asks me to stay. Pip hesitates, but I go straight into the café. Maisie strokes my neck.

'Aren't you lovely?' she says. 'Phil always keeps

a bowl of water down for dogs, don't you, Phil?'

The man we followed down the road nods his head and smiles.

'What can I get you?' he says to Pip.

A new family! I want him to say, but Pip has become awkward and stutters.

'Er – w-what can I have for fifty pence?'

'Chocolate brownie and a glass of apple juice any good to you?'

Pip nods, standing still as if he's glued to the floorboards.

'I'll bring it over to you if you want to go and sit by the window,' says Maisie.

The café walls are lined with pictures and paintings of animals, and the tables and chairs have been painted like leopards and tigers and zebras, with spots and stripes. I feel quite at home here. It is warm and I'm enjoying listening to the hum of voices, the coffee machine gurgling on the counter and Phil or Maisie calling, 'Who ordered the Spanish omelette?' or 'Hot chocolate, anyone?'

I am lying under the table out of the way, watching Pip's feet tapping up and down. He's nervous and excited and I wonder when he's going to say something. He makes his chocolate brownie last what seems like hours. I wonder what's going through his mind. How's he going to break the news to Phil that he is his son? And what will Phil say? He's already got a son, called Sam, he'd said. How weird will this be? All these things might be going through Pip's mind. What's going through my mind is whether or not someone will give me something to eat, and the smell of the person who has been at this table before. It's a beachcombing sort of smell. It makes me think of sitting under the pier with Pip, eating our saveloy and chips. Because I can smell chips too. My paws feel sweaty. I realise I'm more nervous than I thought.

The café is busy all morning. People discuss things. Laugh. Exclaim. And it's very loud listening to a lot of people crunching their biscuits and swallowing their food. There is a gradual changeover from breakfast to lunch, and then it becomes even more busy with a small queue beginning to form outside. Maisie comes over with a cloth and wipes the table. She smiles at Pip.

'Can I get you anything else?'

Pip shakes his head.

'Would you mind if we had your table then? We're a bit short at the moment.'

Pip jumps up immediately.

'Er . . . sorry,' he mumbles, and I also leap to my feet. Is he going to do it now? In front of all these people? But Pip just says 'Thank you' to Phil, who lifts a hand in acknowledgement and we push past the little queue and out into the street.

Then Pip starts to run. He's running and skipping and I'm running and skipping and jumping too. 'What's going on, Pip?' I say.

'I've got to get some money so that I can go back into the café,' he says. 'Otherwise I don't know how to see him.'

I think Pip's daft. Not that I don't love him – I do. But really, all he has to do is go back in the café, maybe when it's a bit quieter, and tell his dad *who he is*.

'Or we can follow him home again,' I say hopefully.

We walk around the town. It's pretty similar to the last one. I think these seaside places were all built by the same person. We find the library. This is obviously where Pip is happiest. And where Pip is happiest, so am I. There is a cardboard box to the side of the building with tattered paperbacks in. Pip rummages through and produces one. He sits on the steps and reads. I know my job. I lie down, my head on my paws. I follow each passer-by with my eyes. If only I could juggle or eat fire or do something *impressive*.

For some time there is nothing in Pip's hat. Then a young man tosses a few coins in. I am waiting for the librarian to come down the steps and ask us to move. But no one disturbs us. A little further along, a guy is selling a newspaper.

'*Big Issue*, madam? *Big Issue*, sir?' I'm pleased to see he doesn't have a dog. I'm wondering now, as I can't juggle, if Pip ought to be selling something.

A clock somewhere strikes four and I've had to shut my eyes. I didn't get much sleep under the bush and all the excitement has tired me out. I open them again when I hear a coin land in Pip's hat. I look up. It's the girl with the pink hair from the café.

She smiles at Pip and stops to stroke my head. I can smell coffee and cakes.

'Hello again!' she says.

'Oh, hi!' says Pip.

'You came into the café, didn't you?'

Pip nods.

'I did an early shift today, so Phil's let me home early. It's nice there, isn't it? Phil's a friend of my mum's and he offered me the job when he first opened up. Did you like the chocolate brownies? My mum makes them.'

Pip nods and grins at her. I think he likes Maisie. And so do I. She looks kind and has a little silver stud in her nose and chatty earrings.

'What's he like then, this Phil?' asks Pip, trying to sound casual.

'Oh, he's a lovely man. He's so generous and friendly.'

'What time does the café close?'

'He shuts about six. On Saturdays Mum comes

and helps him and we open for supper. It's even busier then. You're new round here, aren't you? Where you living?'

Pip looks awkward and shrugs his shoulders.

'There's a youth hostel round the corner if you're looking for somewhere. Go back past the café, cross the main road and it's the other side of town. I've gotta go. See ya!'

'See ya!' says Pip.

The streetlights are coming on but everything seems rather dull now that Maisie's gone. Pip picks up his hat, pockets the money and says to me, 'Come on, let's find somewhere to stay. I'll talk to Dad tomorrow.'

The café looks as if it's quietening down as we go back past, and Pip and I can't resist a quick look inside. Phil is chatting to a table of customers.

It takes us ages to find the youth hostel and when we get there the man behind the desk says, 'No dogs!'

He doesn't even say sorry!

I know Pip won't leave me so there's no point

in trying to persuade him to stay. Besides, I don't want anyone else to take me home, thinking I'm a stray. It says quite clearly that I'm not. PIP and RAY. PIP and RAY, it says on my tag. So HANDS OFF!

The café is closed when we walk past but Phil is sitting at a table on his own, doing his accounts. This is it. This is it. Pip's going to do something. I just know it. We've got nowhere to stay and we might as well take our chance. But he just stands by the window, looking in. Well I'm going to do something then, I decide. I go to the door, jump up against it and bark.

'Let us in!'

I can see Phil lift his head and then shake it. He goes back to his paperwork.

I try again. This time he notices Pip and gets up and unlocks the door.

'We're closed, I'm afraid,' he says.

'Are you . . . Are you Phillip Seagrove?' Pip says. I thought we *knew* he was Phillip Seagrove.

'Yes?' he answers enquiringly.

'I'm Pip Henderson.'

Pip Henderson!

I thought *he* was Phillip Seagrove too. He told that farmer . . . And then it dawns on me how stupid I am. *Of course.* He just told the farmer the first name that popped into his head. And his head has been full of his dad.

Phil looks as if he ought to know who Pip Henderson is, but can't quite recall.

Pip takes the photo out of his pocket and shows it to him. 'This is you. Isn't it?'

Phil takes the picture and puts on his glasses. 'Yes! Where did you get this?'

'My mum gave it to me.'

'Your mum? Who's your mum?'

'Janie. Janie Henderson . . .'

I can hear Pip faltering. Please don't give up now, I think. You've got this far. You've got to keep going.

'Janie Henderson! Your mum! My goodness, how is she? I haven't seen her in years! Where's she living now?'

'Mum's dead.'

Phil's face sort of creases up.

'Oh no,' he says. 'That's awful. How? How did she die?'

'Cancer.'

And as he says that word Pip's shoulders begin to shake and I look up and see two large tears rolling down his face and now his whole body is shaking and he is crying.

Phil puts his hand on Pip's shoulder. And then a strange look comes over his face. It is a mixture of concern and curiosity and fear.

'I'm so sorry,' he says, guiding Pip into the café. 'Come on in and sit down for a moment and you can tell me all about her.'

Chapter 11

I sit under the table. For a moment, till Pip stops crying, nothing is said. I lick his ankle so he knows I'm still here and give him an encouraging whimper.

I peek out and see Phil, standing by the counter, the curious look still on his face.

'How old are you?' Phil asks.

'Fourteen.'

And then there is a long silence and I can hear everyone's hearts beating in their chests, including mine, and I hear Phil whisper under his breath, 'Oh my God!' and then he pulls back a chair and sits down at the table.

Then I listen to them talking.

Talk. Talk.

Pip tells his dad things and Phil tells Pip things and they talk.

Talk. Talk. And now I'm thinking of Pip's mum. Janie. Janie. Jane. Now *there's* a familiar name. Who was Jane? And for some odd reason the picture of a crown pops into my head. But I can't think why.

I hear Phil ring home and speak to his wife.

'I'm going to be a bit late back. Something extraordinary has happened. I'll tell you about it later. Is Sam all right?'

Then Phil's on the phone again. 'Maisie? Can I have a word with your mum? No, it's not about the chocolate brownies. It's a lot more important than that!'

About twenty minutes later, a woman who looks like Maisie, but without the pink hair or the stud in the nose, gently knocks on the door.

'Sal!' Phil says. 'Thanks for coming round. I want you to meet someone special.'

He puts his arm round Pip's shoulders.

'This is my – er – son. Pip!'

My son Pip! I feel all warm and glowing. I want him to be my dad too.

I don't know Sal but I can tell she's surprised.

'Does Viv know?' she says. 'About Pip?' she adds, in case there might be some confusion.

'Well, yes . . . no . . . I haven't told her yet. It'll be a bit of a shock. I didn't know, you see – about Pip. And so I need to talk everything through with her.'

He hesitates for a moment.

'So – can you help me? I can't just walk in with Pip and say, "This is my son." Could you take him back with you tonight, so he has somewhere to stay? Then I'll have a proper chance to talk things over with Viv. I know this is a lot to ask . . .'

Sal hesitates for a moment. Then says, 'Yes – I can do that. Have you had any supper yet, Pip?'

Pip shakes his head. 'Can Ray come too?'

'Who's Ray?'

'My dog, of course.'

And I poke my head out from underneath the table and Sal laughs.

'Oh, yes!' she says, smiling for the first time. 'He can certainly come.'

'I'm a she,' I tell her.

I'm glad that Sal is fine about me spending the night with Pip. I know he needs me more than ever tonight.

I've never slept on a bed before! It is *so* comfy and I curl up in the crook of Pip's knees and he puts his hand on my head and whispers goodnight to me and I wonder if this will be our last night together because I have no idea what Viv will say.

In the morning, Maisie goes off to work at Café Zoo and Pip and I hang around the kitchen while Sal cooks us breakfast. They are vegetarians, but she still manages a good cooked breakfast. Grilled tomatoes, fried mushrooms, eggs and vegetarian sausages. Because she wasn't expecting a dog to stay, there aren't any bone-shaped biscuits (thank goodness), so I get a couple of the sausages. Really, they are quite nice, considering that they don't have any meat in them.

The phone rings about nine o'clock and I hear Sal saying, 'Yes. Yes. Really? Good. Yes. Yes. I'll do that. Good. OK. Bye!'

She turns to Pip.

'Phillip says he's going to shut the café early today and you can stay here, as he's still sorting some stuff out. I'm to take you there later on this afternoon.'

Pip is looking nervous now. 'Do you think it's going to be OK?'

Sal smiles at him. 'I'm *sure* it's going to be OK. Now there's a big jazz-music festival on in the town today – people come for miles – so there'll be plenty to look at and listen to. Shall I show you the way to the beach so that you can walk Ray and then you can wander round the town? Can you find your way back here for about four o'clock, do you think?'

Pip nods. I think he's looking rather pale. He needs some fresh air and so do I. I've been here under the table for too long and I need to stretch my legs.

It's a blustery day outside. I'm sure it's going to be good for Pip. Why shouldn't his dreams come true?

Sniff! Sniff! Seaweed, plastic bottles, beach

shoes. I am assaulted by smells. My sense of smell has escalated and my hearing too. I can hear food hit a feeding bowl from more than twenty paces now. I can hear a baby cry in the next street. A couple argue. A car engine starts up. A tin can rattles along the pavement.

Hang on. Hang on.

Where's Pip now? Has he gone? Has he left me alone on the beach? But there he is – throwing pebbles into the sea. How pleased I am to see him. As if I haven't seen him all day.

We wander back into the town. There seem to be flags and bunting everywhere and on almost every street corner there's a busker playing some instrument or other. On the green are a couple of marquees and people are cramming into them, trying to hear the music. I don't know why they bother – you can hear it perfectly well from out here.

Pip is not himself. He keeps sighing and looking at his watch. We sit down on the grass.

'I don't know, Ray,' he says to me. 'I don't think that this will work out. Why didn't he come and collect us this morning and take us back to meet Viv? I expect they've had a huge fight over it and Viv has threatened to leave if he brings us back home, and he hasn't got the – the courage to tell us. I can't bear to hear him tell me we can't live with them. I think we should go. We might as well go, cos he obviously doesn't want us.'

I look at Pip and a huge tear rolls down his cheek. He sniffs and angrily wipes it away. I don't mind him crying but I do mind him giving up hope.

'We've got to stay, Pip,' I tell him. 'If we go we'll never know and you'll spend your whole life wondering what might have happened.'

I push up to his face and rub my wet nose against his cheek and he lies back on the grass and looks at the sky. The whole picture, Pip, I think to myself. See the whole picture – don't worry about the missing bits.

I see a woman pushing a man in a wheelchair. There is a golden dog at their side, wearing a coat with letters written on it. He looks smart.

'Sit, Dunbar!' I can hear the woman say.

She looks flushed, as if she's having difficulties negotiating the wheelchair through all the people. I'd like to go and help her. She looks like someone who might need my help. But then I look at Dunbar, the golden dog, and think that he could probably do a million more things than I to help. I feel jealous. For a moment, I want to be that dog with the anxious-looking woman.

For some reason, my tail gives a little wag. The woman looks nice; there is something familiar about her. She looks kind as well as anxious. She takes a locket out from round her neck and twists it through her fingers. Then she rests her hand on the man's shoulder and smiles at him. The man lifts his head and smiles back and I suddenly feel all warm inside. I think I might know her. I can't see the man's face now. He is sitting very still with his head bent again.

I am watching the dog. He is very still too. Perhaps he can do other things because it doesn't look as if he's being any help at all. I feel silly now. Because I want a coat like that too. I'd like to have a yellow coat with letters written on it.

Perhaps Pip will buy me a yellow coat with letters on when it gets colder.

Pip has sat up and seen the dog too.

'Look, Ray! There's a dog wearing a Dogs for the Disabled coat. I bet he's clever!' Then he bends down and gives me a hug.

'But not as clever as *you*! You're the best dog in the world. And if Dad's wife doesn't want us – well, I have *you*, and we'll find a way to get by.'

I give him a big lick. I think he's putting on a brave face.

We walk near them and the woman makes me think of hot buttered toast and warm baths and perfumed hugs and boiled eggs with soldiers. I am feeling something but I don't know what it is. It's something to do with the locket. I've seen someone do that before but I can't think who. It makes my heart stop beating for a moment. When it starts up again I can feel the blood rush from my head, taking the memory of the locket with it.

'What's up, Ray?' Pip asks.

But I don't answer him because I've got nothing to say.

The sad woman with the dog. The faceless man in the wheelchair. A boy upstairs on a bus. The house in – what avenue was it? I can only recall Marjorie's little house at the top of Barton Road. It's like they're all inside an egg-timer and someone has tipped it upside down and they're slipping through to the bottom of the glass.

Going.

When we get back, Pip helps Sal make the brownies for the café and then it's four o'clock and time to go.

'It'll be all right, Pip,' I tell him. 'He seems a nice man to have as a dad and he might give you a job in the café!'

Phil has already put the CLOSED sign up at the door when we arrive and I can see Maisie inside, wiping down the tables. Phil smiles at us and gives Pip a huge hug. This looks like a good sign to me. Maisie takes off her apron and, putting on her coat, gives us a wave.

'Bye, you guys! See you soon!'

We sit down at the table by the window again.

'Do you want a drink, Pip? Apple juice? Orange juice? I can make you a hot chocolate if you like?' asks Phil.

But Pip shakes his head. He just wants to *know*.

'You can imagine how surprised I was when you turned up, Pip,' Phil starts saying. 'I had no idea that Janie was pregnant. She didn't tell me, you know. She moved away as soon as college was over and never told me where she'd gone. I hope she managed all right. I'd hate to think of her struggling.'

In between asking more questions about Pip's mum, he tells Pip about Viv and how, although shocked at first, she really wants to meet him. I watch Pip's foot sliding up and down the leg of his chair and I know he's still worried that Viv will not like him when she does finally get to meet him.

I can see a piece of toast that someone must have dropped under the next table and has escaped Maisie's beady eye. I begin, very slowly, to edge myself towards it. Elbow. Elbow. Foot. Foot. Body. Mmmm.

There're some good smells coming from behind the counter too. I don't think anyone will notice if I go and check them out. Pip and his dad seem to have a lot to talk about.

There's a bin and a bucket round the back of the counter. Scraps of bacon, toast, some omelette. All smelling pretty good. The bin is too tall to get into so I have to jump up. But it slips away from me and falls on my head.

'Aargh!' I say and scuttle back to Pip's feet.

'Ray!' he says. 'Bad dog! You mustn't do that!'

Bad dog? He's never called me *that* before. I'm a hungry dog, that's all. I suppose he doesn't want his dad to think I'm always going around tipping bins over.

I move from Pip's feet and sit under another table. They carry on talking. Bad dog, indeed. I feel the corners of my mouth turn down and I sigh.

I'm not listening to them any more. I'm just protecting Pip. I like his dad and if he takes us in I dare say I'll be protecting him as well. And this Viv woman and Sam. I'd better brush up my protecting skills. The snake man might walk into the café at any moment. I'm starting right now.

Then we're all up on our feet and going out of the café and down the street and back to the mauve house with the blue door. I have to check that our bicycle is still there and it is. Pip seems to have forgotten about it. That's another thing I'll have to keep an eye out for.

I miss the introductions at the door because another dog has been at the gate. But there is Viv, a tall, smiling woman with dark hair, giving Pip a hug, and she smells of kindness and kisses and generosity.

'Hello!' she says to me. 'Now, let's have a proper look at you. Ah yes. You look a kind dog. You'll be nice to our Sam, won't you?'

And I know that, as long as he's not like Cyril, I'll take very good care of him.

We're in the house now. There seems to be a lot going on. Piles of books and newspapers. A bicycle in the hall. Paintings on the walls. Toys on the floor and, best of all, there is Sam. And he's my height! Small and fair-haired, he waddles towards me on his little chubby legs.

'Doggie!' he says and he puts his arms around me and lays his head on my neck. I wag my tail, but ever so gently because I don't want to knock him over.

I don't sleep with Pip any more. I have my own basket and my own rug – tartan: black and red checks. It is warm by the stove. I have my own bowl to eat out of and my own bowl to drink out of. Then there are Sam's toys and *my* toys and sometimes Sam and I get a bit muddled and he's playing with my rubber chicken and I'm chewing on his toy duck. At night I lie awake, making sure nothing happens to anyone in the house – which is a HUGE responsibility as there are so many of them. I am particularly protecting them against the snake man. I get my rest in the day, when I can see that everyone is OK and that no one has died in their sleep.

Pip works with Maisie at the café and sometimes I look after them all there and sometimes I look after Sam and Viv at home. And Pip takes me for walks on the beach. More often than not Maisie comes too. I'm always pleased to see Maisie with her smells of joy and laughter and hope.

And one day I saved Sam's life.

We were all out on the pavement and Viv was talking to her neighbour and Sam had toddled off and was examining something in the middle of the road. I could hear something. I couldn't see it but I could hear it. It was the engine of a car and it was being driven far too fast. *Screech. Scream. Roar.* It still hadn't come into view but I sensed it. And this is what must be meant by having a sixth sense because it was a very strong feeling and I just had to do something about it.

'Viv! Watch out for Sam!' I shouted and I got hold of her skirt and I tugged it so that she would stop talking to her neighbour and then I ran into the road and I pushed Sam with my nose to make him get up and I told him, in no uncertain terms, that he had to get out of the road NOW! Of course, he just giggled at me, even though he knew what I was saying. But Viv had seen. And now the car was coming round the bend on two wheels and she ran into the road and scooped Sam up and we both raced back onto the pavement and the car tore past us and disappeared over the brow of the hill.

'Oh, Sam, you naughty boy!' she scolded him. 'You must never go into the road.'

And Sam started to cry and I gave him a lick to tell him it was all right really, but that his mum was right to get cross. And the neighbour gave me a pat and said, 'I reckon that dog of yours saved his life with all that barking.'

And Viv gave me a big hug.

Chapter 12

We are all around the table having a late breakfast.

I know there is someone there even before the door bell rings. But Sam is feeding me some of his toast under the table so I don't take much notice. Normally I'd be the first at the door going, 'Someone at the door! Come on – open up!' but today I don't want to leave this tasty morsel so I let someone else go.

I hear a woman's voice. She sounds familiar.

'I'm so sorry to be a nuisance. Is this where the Seagroves live?'

'Yes,' says Viv. 'May I help you?'

'I just wondered if a lovely boy called Pip had managed to find your house and what had happened to him?'

I practically choke on the toast in my hurry to get out from under the table and get to that door. There are a lot of legs in the way.

'Marjorie! Marjorie! It's me, Ray! Yes! We made it! We made it! Have you come back for your bicycle?'

'Oh,' she says, bending down. 'How lovely! Ray! You *did* find Pip's dad after all!'

I am so excited I have to go and tell Pip, but he's heard her voice too and is walking towards the door.

'Marjorie! You've come to see us!' Then I see a look of guilt pass over his face. 'Oh, I should have told you! I'm so sorry – after all you did for us. I just didn't think! And Dad's told the authorities and it's all proper now and – oh, I'm so happy to see you!' Pip gives Marjorie a big hug, then, remembering his manners, he introduces her.

'Viv, Dad – this lady saved us from horrible food poisoning and gave us your address.'

'And she lent us her bicycle,' I add. Really, Pip seems to have forgotten all about that bicycle.

'You must come in then!' says Phil, with a big smile on his face. 'I have a lot to thank you for.'

'I brought you some letters I hadn't got round to forwarding on to you. In case,' she added, 'you didn't know what I was talking about.'

Then they all go inside and sit round the table and I help clear the plates by giving them a lick, which I know I shouldn't but they are busy talking and they haven't noticed me anyway.

Later I go and sit on the floor between Marjorie and Pip. Perhaps Marjorie could come and live here too. I'd really like that.

'Any time you want to go on holiday and you can't take Ray,' she says, 'I'm very happy to have her, you know. While you are away.' I push my nose under her hand and give her a lick. I'm collecting quite a family now.

'Oh, by the way, Pip,' Marjorie continues, 'they caught the fellow who took my car. The police have been after him for ages. He was well known for stealing almost anything. In his photograph he looked the most unpleasant man. And he had – you know – *tattoos*. He's locked up in prison now, thank goodness.'

Locked up in prison? A huge sense of relief passes through my body. One less thing to worry about. Protecting everyone against the snake man had been a very tiresome business.

Marjorie often visits us now. She particularly likes taking me for a walk when Viv goes out with Sam in the pushchair. They all talk a lot. I don't listen much any more. I don't understand most of it. There are words which are important, though, that I listen out for. Words like *Let's go for a walk* and *Dinnertime, Ray!* And there are things that I would never do. Like I would never take a treat from anyone if they had asked me to leave it alone.

There are lots of people in my life now. Pip and his family and Maisie and Sal and Jack and Marjorie. I know we don't see Jack, but I still feel he's there. And I always keep a lookout for him. In case he's round the next corner or walking towards us along the road. Apart from

Pip, who obviously is Number One, the person I like being with best is Sam. Little Sam with his laughter and tears. Sam who cannot talk yet. Well, not properly. He can say *Mum* and *Dad* and *Pip* and *Doggie* and *toy* and *drinkie*, which is more than me.

And I know something about Sam that no one else does. I know that Sam understands me perfectly well.

I used to tell him things about myself and he knew what I was saying. And he would tell me things back. Like *No one understands me!* And *How long do I have to wait for my tea?* And *Oh no, it's bathtime again!* And all the time he gurgles and gabbles and makes funny noises, I understand him perfectly well too. But the curious thing is, the more he is able to speak the other humans' language, the less he is able to speak mine.

He's saying quite a lot now.

I'm sleeping more. When I dream, flashes of people I don't know come into my sleep. I don't dream about people I know.

There's a boy, sitting on top of a bus. He looks nice, but not as nice as Pip. He's there again, playing football. Then there is a man and a woman, a bit like Phil and Viv. In my dream I like them but I don't know who they are. The woman is always cooking me meals and giving me hugs. Then there is a girl. I don't know who she is either, but she's nearly always in my dreams. I'd like to know her. She is friendly and kind and in the dreams she is always *doing* things. In one dream she is flying a kite and I'm there too. Trying to fly the kite with her. And when it falls to the ground we both laugh and we both run over and pick it up and try to fly it again.

Whenever I see Pip or Sam or Phil or Viv it's like I haven't seen them in a very long time. Particularly Pip. I'm always so pleased to set eyes on him. My sense of time has become very muddled now. For instance, it always seems like it should be time for a meal or a little snack.

The weather is warming up and Pip and Maisie are sitting together on the sand and I'm standing by the edge of the sea. There's something really interesting, half buried in the sand. I just have to go and unearth it.

Yes! I thought so. A piece of wood.

I pick it up and run over to Pip, dropping it by his side. He ruffles my ears but makes no attempt to get up and throw it for me. I take it round to Maisie but all she does is play with the wood and idly buries it again by her side. I go back to the sea. *Splash*, *splash*, the water is swirling around my legs. Warm and silky.

I look across the horizon. I walk a little way into the water's edge. I look behind me. Pip and Maisie are still sitting in the sand, chatting away to each other. I start to swim. I can hear, just faintly, above the lapping of the waves and the seagulls screaming by the cliffs, a voice. Calling me.

'Daisy! Daisy! Come in now!'

I am swimming into the waves and I think of Pip on his birthday when he said it was like going back into the womb. The water is warm and there is a voice again. Calling. Calling.

A wave washes over me and there is my room in Alexander Avenue with the mattress on the floor and the 'Save the Planet' posters on the walls, and the water now is all pink and swirly like my mosquito net. And there is Jessica Warner and Owen Taylor and Miss Roberts, the games teacher, all waving at me.

They're all out there. Mum and Dad and Jack too. And it's Mum's voice I can hear.

'Daisy! Daisy! Come in! The water's really warm!'

Another wave splashes over my head.

Then I'm in the car with Dad. And Mum is at the door calling to us, in her 'I'm the Boss' apron. 'Don't forget to buy some cheese biscuits!' And we're out on the road now. And Dad turns to me and says, 'Could you just check that my wallet's on the back seat, Daisy?' And I unbuckle my seat belt and turn to look and there's the wallet. Brown and worn, with my scarf and Dad's hat. And I turn back and something huge and black blots out the light. It is a horse jumping over the hedge. I look in wonder as it clears the hedge and I hear Dad shouting and I see fear in the horse's eyes.

And then there's a noise like crashing, crumpling metal and everywhere are diamonds catching the light. Diamonds in my hair and in my face and I'm flying now.

Weightless.

Nothing.

Dark. Empty nothing.

Crashing. Crashing.

It is waves crashing around my head.

Turn round. Swim back to shore. Look around.

There he is.

Walking towards me. Along the beach.

Calling my name.

'Ray! Ray!'

Ears. Bark. Tail wag.

Run.

Stop.

Happy. Happy. Happy.

My Pip.

Here.

Acknowledgements

The Dog, Ray brought my agent, Suzy Jenvey, and I together. All thanks to her for believing in it from the very beginning. Also Emma Matthewson, my lovely editor, and all at Hot Key who have helped Ray to finally wag her tail on the page. Huge thanks to Elinor Bagenal who encouraged me so much with the writing of it and who put me in touch with Suzy. Also Serita Lewis whose amazing photographs of people living on the streets were truly informative, and her knowledge – and that of some *Big Issue* sellers – helped me with writing about Pip and Jack. Johnny Bull and Susie Alexander, for reading it before anyone else and helping me with ideas and improvements. And finally to our own dog, Beezle, who was the inspiration. He let me into the ways of dogs.

About the Author

Linda Coggin taught horse riding in the West Indies before studying mime in Paris and Czechoslovakia. As part of a small company, she played the fringe theatres and cabaret circuits of Europe. She appeared in Ken Russell's film *Gothic* as the mechanical doll. She worked as an actor for several years and presented *The Home Show* for Thames Television.

Linda writes and performs her own poetry, and her debut novel *The Boy with the Tiger's Heart* was published in 2014. She lives in Wiltshire with her two children and numerous animals. Follow Linda at www.lindacogsblog.blogspot.co.uk.

Thank you for choosing a Hot Key book.

If you want to know more about our authors and what we publish, you can find us online.

You can start at our website

www.hotkeybooks.com

And you can also find us on:

We hope to see you soon!